John Dover's

A Fistful of Fangs

Published by: Lights Out Creative Press, LLC

ISBN: 979-8-9986261-3-5

Novels

Danger in Bass Clef

A Song for Charlie

Runners Blues

Once Upon a Fang in the West

Comic Books

Johnny Scotch four part mini series

Anthologies and Collaborations

Monsters 'N' Things ('N' Things Anthology book 2)

Tales From the Braided Pony

Carnival of Horror (A Carnival Themed Horror Anthology)

100 Word Horrors Book 1 & 2 (Collections of Horror Drabbles)

Tenebrous

The Phone

Marti's Music Kitchen Cookbook

Trumpet Method

The Intentional Trumpeter

To Jessica. Your patience and support over the years has made it possible for me to continue to create these wild worlds. None of this would exist without your love and creative inspiration.

The Stagecoach

1

Juliette's eyes itched. Wisps of dust leeched into the stagecoach through the flimsy, rattling door's seam. She stared blankly out the window. The jagged scenery obscured into a beige blur as the coach pushed forward. She kept her attention on the dusty landscape, avoiding the furtive glances from the man seated across from her. His eyes reminded her of her husband. It had been months since his passing, but the ache of loss still haunted her. The numbness in her heart reflected in the pallid palette of the barren landscape.

The stark countryside rolled by. Dust-riddled hill sides peppered with sagebrush all bled into one another. Juliette relented to a trance-like state and ignored the pangs of nostalgia that threatened to bring her back to the day she found her husband slumped over the plow. Nothing could be done. The doctor had told her his heart just stopped.

She stayed on the farmstead for a short time, but there was nothing there for her anymore. Working the land was his dream. Her dreams of raising a family had been soured by multiple miscarriages. But they loved and supported each other, and he continued his drive to transform the fruitless earth they had found into the fertile farm he always dreamt of.

They had traveled across the country to start their life together and without John, she couldn't imagine tending the arid land of his dreams. She sold the plot and most of their belongings to buy passage to the coast. She hoped to start over and reimagine her life without him. The few things she kept were her clothes, some pieces of jewelry left to her by her dead mother in case she needed to sell something for money down the line, and her one gift from John on their wedding day: A vanity kit comprising a handheld mirror, a brush, and a hair pin, all crafted from solid silver. Her one worldly treasure, tucked away in a steamer trunk that rattled against the roof of the compartment that was ferrying her across the unforgiving Southwestern desert.

The wooden coach resonated with the crunch of the metal framed wheels bouncing along the gravel-riden path. Cargo and passengers alike bobbed and bounced along with the jarring motion of the road, their discomfort eased by the worn, but well-padded seats and walls protecting them from the elements. The rutted route, carved by the hundreds of trips along the rust tinted stone formations of the desolate pass, guided the coach drivers no matter the weather or time of day.

The day had been long and dry allowing for their course to be unimpeded by the softening of the ground that the rain brought on. The horses had been switched out almost forty miles prior and glistened and grunted from exertion as they pushed forward through the final miles of their journey.

Chester sat atop the bouncing coach, grizzled and gruff, hunched forward by years of being battered by the trail and the weather, wind-strained eyes trained on the horizon. His chin was moist with the brown stain of chaw clinging to the grey and yellowed whiskers of his bristled jaw line. The old coot knew the route well enough to drive it in the dark, and his protégé, a young man of about nineteen, with little knowledge of the world beyond the carriage that numbed his backside day in and day out, sat lookout. A scattergun rested erect on his knee. They were used to the relentless pace of the trail and had been pushing their chariot with little more than a few hours rest a day for the past two weeks. With the final miles before them, the promise of rest kept them focused on the task at hand as was expected by those who paid to ride.

Inside the coach, a mismatched group of travelers wearily swayed back and forth maintaining a polite quiet. A buttoned-up aristocrat and his dutiful wife. A slick, fast-talking gambler named Levi who was more familiar with the lady folk than was generally accepted by polite society. And Juliette, dressed in widow's black from head to toe, in honor of her late husband.

The coach had driven without a stop for the past six hours, covering the terrain at an unrelenting pace. Chester was in a hurry to make the next town before dark, eager to get a jump on a week's rest. Their destination was home to a saloon of renown that would keep him and his young mentee in whiskey and perfume laced petticoats for the duration. Both he and the boy were anxious to partake in the rest and recreation that awaited them. With only fifteen miles to go, they pushed the horses hard as the sun dove for the horizon.

"Sun's starting to dip, Chester. You think we'll make it?" The young man said, spitting the words past a thick coating of grit and dust.

"It'll be close, but it won't be too dark before we pull in. Just settle yer britches." Chester's rasping voice cut through the din of the rattling wheels.

"I hate riding in the dark."

"It ain't the first time we've been out past yer bedtime, won't be the last."

"It's not my bedtime, ya onery old cuss. There just won't be no girls left if we get in much later than sundown."

"You do realize that weren't no girl last time, right?"

"No need to lash out just cuz you ain't been able to get your knob wet shootin' blanks like you is."

Chester whooped. His young companion had been honing his banter under his tutelage and he was proud of the quick quips he had been stringing together of late.

"Just see if you can make it out with a few coins left in your purse this time. I ain't buyin' your meals for another week like the last time."

The coach drivers' competitive chortles accompanied the nights dark purple hue as it chased the gentle pale blue of day beyond the horizon.

Inside the dusty carriage, the riders were restless and eager to be freed from the compartment's jostling, able to partake in a good night's lodging and meal. Little conversation had been had since they started off. Pleasantries and polite nods were exchanged when they loaded up allowing for awkward, but accepted apologies from the gentle collisions the bumpy ride had provided throughout their journey.

"Jameson," Mary, his wife, broke the silence, startling the slick-dressed man across the way out of a nap as she inquired of her husband.

Jameson cleared his throat and turned to his wife. "Yes, Mare?"

"How much longer do you suppose we will be?"

"We must be starting to get close. We've been going hard for quite a while. Why, my dear?"

Mary blushed as she didn't want to appear improper to her traveling companions. "Oh, no real reason my love. Just in need of a stretch of my legs and a…" Mary glanced sheepishly across to her other traveling companions and leaned in closer to Jameson's ear, "powder."

"Ahh. I'm sure it won't be long but if you need me to rouse the attention of our driver, I'm sure—"

"Oh no, no." Mary waved him off sheepishly, "I don't want to be a bother." She bowed her head to hide the rising blush on her round cheeks.

The slick-dressed man gave a sly, knowing smile but did not prod Jameson or Mary to speak up.

Juliette bade no heed to the hushed conversation across from her. Between extended gazes into the dusty reach and her time devouring the book she had been gifted before the journey by her aunt, she remained distracted from the quibbles around her. Already, the inside of the carriage was dimming, and she could barely make out the words scrambled by the jostling of their ride. Frustrated, she closed the book and turned her attention to the growing shadows of dusk that escorted them along their journey.

She looked to the dim glow emerging from behind the hills that was trading places with the sinking sun. The full moon teased its appearance as the sun dipped its toe behind the mountains. Juliette felt she could trace her fingers across its surface it was so large this evening. The kind of moon that you could reach out and pluck from the sky like a ripe apple. As the shadows melded with the growing dark of dusk, fresh shapes leaned away from the growing light of the moon, reaching out to mingle with the coming night.

Billowing dust erupted up from the wheels as they pounded down on the dry trail. Juliette scanned the darkening landscape for shapes. She questioned her tired vision swearing she saw a boulder that appeared to dart away as they passed by. There were no bison out this way, and a wild horse would look less rounded. Her tired eyes must have played a trick on her from the long day of reading and getting bounced around in her skull, trying to keep track of the dancing ink on the page.

The stagecoach shuddered violently. The screech of metal and the splintering of wood drowned out the frantic cries inside the carriage. The carriage quaked, its rear left wheel torn away. Jimmy flew from his seat, hitting the ground and skidding to a halt just clear of the toppling stagecoach. Chester clamored to keep control of the horses as he pulled back on the reins, bracing himself on the floorboards below him. The leather reins constricted his hands. He yelped as the knuckles on his right hand strained and popped under the pressure of the panicked horses fighting the out-of-control carriage.

Inside, the four passengers were thrown together in a mess of flailing limbs and terror-stricken screams. Levi was crushed between the other three and the corner of the compartment he had been in. The rock-encrusted ground crunched by, spitting gravel into the compartment, stinging any exposed flesh. Levi grimaced as his shoulder was pressed against the open window and ground against the sharp road as the carriage completed its journey and settled on its side. Chester tumbled forward, still holding the reins as he brought the horses to a halt under the weight of the fallen payload.

2

The coach was filled with the pained groans of its dazed passengers. The damaged carriage settled on its side, the weight of its cargo and passengers holding it down after skidding to a halt. The wheel that remained slowly spun, grinding and squeaking to a stop. Chester inspected his horses. Aside from their nervous chuffs, they had escaped the wreck with no real damage.

Jimmy made his way back to the carriage. He climbed up the underside finding footholds amongst the damaged undercarriage to steady his path. He cleared the edge and climbed atop the side of the carriage and peered down at the mass of bodies clumped together inside.

"Everyone still movin' in there?" Jimmy said, leaning in through the window and pulling the door open. His left leg ached from his fall, but it was more a nuisance than debilitating.

"Moving, yes. Mostly in one piece. Jesus! Watch those elbows!" Levi yelped from the bottom of the pile.

The rest of the group squirmed around on top of him, working to right themselves without doing more damage to those beneath them as they found their footing on the door that was now a floor.

Jimmy reached in and helped swing legs free and grabbed hold of the nearest and least tangled set of hands he could find. The carriage rocked as the passengers, one by one, were extracted from the off-kilter compartment. They each navigated their way down to the ground fumbling for the most dignified way to fall on their rumps.

"Horses are all okay. A bit spooked, but they'll be fine," Chester grumbled as he came around to where the passengers were gathered.

"We're fine, should you care to ask." Mary huffed, brushing dust from the dark fringe of her dress.

"No need to get in a snit, ma'am. We all got shook up and I promise we'll be back on the road in a jiff once we figure out what happened." Chester walked past a flustered Mary as he surveyed the underside of the carriage to figure out the situation.

Mary turned to her husband. "Are you going to let him talk to me that way?"

"I don't think we have much choice, my dear. It's not like this is his fault." Her husband sheepishly turned towards Chester. "Is it sir?" As if looking for a quick answer to satisfy himself and his bride.

Chester sucked on his teeth. "Well, you see here," gesturing to the rear axle and the wheel gently teetering in the air. "That one is fine, but right here," moving his pointed finger down to the side where there should have been a twin for the dangling wheel, "it just plumb ain't there."

The passengers gathered around Chester.

"What do you mean? Where did it go?" Levi asked.

"Ain't right sure. Did anyone see us hit sumpin' a little way back?" Jimmy asked.

Juliette didn't see the wheel hit anything. What she did see, she was not prepared to bring forth to the group for fear of being seen as hysterical. She shook her head slowly with the rest of the passengers.

"Well, fer now, we need to gather all the baggage while there is still a bit of light left. I'll get a fire started and figure out what to do. Since the wheel is gone completely and the carriage is on its side, I'm gonna need a bit of help fixin' us up." Chester pulled out a kerchief from his inside pocket and swabbed the moisture from his forehead.

"Jimmy!" The coach driver hollered over his shoulder.

Jimmy's head popped around the corner. "Yeah!"

"I want you to unhook the horses and take one into town. I'm gonna get things settled here."

"What do I do in town?"

"Go to the livery and tell them we need a wheel brought out here in the morning. Pretty sure they won't do it tonight, and it won't be light enough to work till then anyway." Jimmy wasted no time. He untethered the horse that appeared the most rested. He threw his leg over and gave it an encouraging kick. The two were off.

Chester addressed the passengers: "I'm gonna need the menfolk to do some scroungin' and grab up the cargo before it gets too dark. Me and the ladies will set up a camp here and see if we can figure out some grub."

He looked up to inspect the darkening sky. "Looks like one bit o' luck is with us since there don't seem to be any rain comin' our way."

"You don't expect us to sleep outside, do you?" Mary said.

"Well, I reckon you are welcome to hoof it the rest of the way into town, but it's gonna be a long night for ye," Chester said with an impish rasp to his voice. "Can't lend ya another horse since we will need them fresh for the morning once we get the carriage all fixed up."

"Well, I never." Mary huffed. She turned to her husband to defend her honor and her right to cozier lodgings. He stood by unable to respond. She turned and walked off around the end of the coach to seethe in peace, her stammering husband in pursuit.

3

Night settled over the landscape. The bright orange and tan highlights of the rugged terrain shifted to pale gray, offset by the heavy blue of the darkening sky. The Harvest moon shone bright. Under its pale light, the travelers gathered their lost baggage and cobbled together a rough campsite encircling their fire with the scuffed parcels from the wreck.

Jameson was able to coax Mary back to the safety and comfort of the group. Juliette and Chester built the fire ring and arranged the baggage sturdy enough to sit on or lean against. The growing flames lapped at the night air.

Chester always carried a supply of dried beef and apples for long hauls. The meal would be meager but plentiful enough to fill their bellies for the night as well as again in the morning.

"I can't believe we have to stay out here all night," Mary said. "Couldn't the boy have brought help sooner?"

"He's probably just now getting to Thrall so I can't imagine he would be able to gather the necessary supplies, let alone talk the smithy into trekking this far out in the middle of the night. I know this ain't ideal, but we might as well accept this is where we are." Chester winked at Mary as he ripped a stubborn chunk of dried meat from the hearty piece in his hand.

She scoffed and nibbled on the sour apple cradled in her clutch. She did not like the abrupt old man and was sore at her husband for not coming to her defense.

"Thank you for the food, Chester." Juliette said.

"Least I can do since we're all stuck here tonight." As he nodded to Juliette, a movement just over her shoulder caught his eye.

Levi noticed Chester's gaze and the gentle shift in his facial expression. The rest of the group paid no heed, but Levi, always on the lookout for a tell, picked up on Chester's subtle changes. He was just to the left of the old man, and he adjusted his own sight to find whatever had concerned Chester out in the dark.

Jameson noticed the change in his companions. "What's the matter?" He looked over his own shoulder into the dark where the other two men were fixing their eyes. "Somethin' out there?"

"Some-*thing*." Mary corrected his grammar.

Jameson sighed.

Levi kept his focus on the nearly imperceptible shifts in the inky landscape. There was a mass of black skulking just beyond the light the fire cast around the campsite. The fire made it difficult for their vision to adjust to the details around them. He stood and stepped around the group to the back end of the upended carriage. His eyes adjusted to the dark.

Jameson reached for a loose, heavy branch that lay in the fire. He lifted the torch free from the other logs and moved next to Levi. "What do you see?" He extended the crackling torch in front of them, hoping to illuminate whatever it was Levi was tracking.

"I'm not sure. Ever since the wheel came off, I've been... seein' things."

"Like what?"

"Not sure. Could be the night playing tricks on me, but every time I think I see movement... it stops."

They stood focusing their eyes out past the gentle glow of the campfire and the torch's limited reach.

Mary shifted uneasily by the fire. "You two are scaring me. Please come back. I'm sure there is nothing out there but a coyote."

"Don't sound like a coyote," Chester said.

"She's already scared, you don't have to make it worse, Chester." Juliette scolded the grizzled coot.

He scoffed and returned his attention to the dwindling hunk of dried meat in his hand.

"There it is again." Levi strained his eyes. The amorphous shape in the distance shuddered and shifted quickly to the side, edging closer to the boundary marked by their light.

"You sure? I still don't see nothing."

"Then listen. Whatever it is, it's big. Can't you hear it breathe?"

"I don't hear nothin'."

"Then quit your yappin' and listen." Levi followed the shifting mass as it crept closer. Another few feet and it would reach the torch's light.

"There." Levi slowly raised his arm, directing Jameson's glance to just beyond the light. "Pair of eyes reflecting your light. You see 'em?"

Jameson's torch wobbled, his arm tiring from its weight. "Not sure. Wait a minute. I see them. Jesus." He took a step backward.

Levi grabbed his arm and held him in place. "You move back and it's gonna move towards us. Stay where you are."

"Go to hell. I ain't messin' with that thing."

"We don't even know what it is. It's probably just a coyote checking us out if we are food or not."

"I don't care what it is. I'm going back to the fire. It doesn't seem to like the flames, so I'm staying as close to them as I can." Jameson pried his arm from Levi's grip and backed up to where the others sat. Their attention had turned from their food to what the two men were doing.

Mary fidgeted anxiously. She tugged at Jameson's sleeve. Jameson tossed his torch back to the fire and sat next to her. They nervously watched Levi as he continued to track the shifting shape in the dark.

Levi found that without the torch, he could make out the creature's outline, and he was correct that it would move closer without Jameson swinging the flames around.

Whatever it was, it was getting brave and stalking nearer. Levi's ears perked as he followed the beast's movement. With each step, he heard the crunch of claws scratching across graveled ground. The sound of heavy breaths was clearer as it cautiously closed the distance on its prey. He grew aware that it was much too big to be a coyote or even a wolf. The billowing outline was coming more into focus. The wind shifted. Levi's nostrils twitched at the first whiff of the animal. Its musk was intense. He held his breath so as not to gag on the oily tang that filled the air.

Then it was gone. The bristly form was replaced by the dark gray of rocky ground.

"What the—" Goose flesh rose on the nape of the gambler's neck as adrenaline coursed through his body.

"Is it still there or have you figured out you were seeing things?" Jameson huddled close to his bride. The two of them were edged up against the overturned carriage. Mary clung to Jameson, her nerves getting the best of her.

"It's just gone." Levi scanned the space in front of him from left to right once more, then turned to his travel companions.

"Jesus!" Chester cried out.

"What is it now?" Jameson shot back to the grizzled old

man who stared wide-eyed at him. "Enough with trying to scare the lady folk."

Levi ran toward him, but it was too late. The beast slapped its taloned claw down on Jameson's head, engulfing it in its wiry grip. A spurt of blood shot into the fire with a hiss.

Mary looked at her flailing mate. The fear held her screams back as she followed the shape of the creatures muscled, furry arm up to where it connected to its shoulder. The animal was perched atop the carriage. Jameson's frightful panic barely jostled its girth as it pulled its lips back in a wicked sneer. She screamed, filling the night air with her falsetto screeches.

As if to mock her, the creature leaned forward and let loose a deafening roar, spraying Mary with a slick confetti of spittle.

Levi ran to Jameson, but before he could grab him, Jameson was swiped up and away. The dull thuds of his hands punching at the iron grip around his head faded as the beast retreated into the darkness.

Chester sat frozen, a half-eaten bit of apple hanging from of his jaw. Mary sobbed and called Jameson's name over and over.

Juliette gaped at the spot where Jameson had been. "What was that?"

"Damned if I know. Looked like a wolf, but I never seen a wolf that big, let alone one that moves like that." Levi moved toward the fire and plucked up Jameson's torch. He held it up to see where the creature had been on top of the carriage. There were fresh scuffs from Jameson's struggle as well as indentations where the beast's other hand had held tight to the frame of the upended carriage. "Jesus!"

The party turned toward Jameson's gurgled screams. Soon his cries gave way to the sound of the animal dining noisily in the dark.

Mary crumpled to the ground. Juliette got up and moved to her.

"She okay?" Levi asked.

"No, she's not okay. She just watched her husband get dragged off by some kind of demon." Juliette lifted Mary's head and lay it on her own lap. "She's fainted."

Levi stared in the direction of the chewing sounds, then turned his attention back to the group. "Chester."

The old man didn't respond.

Levi stepped forward. "Chester!"

The disheveled driver started, taking notice of the mess of food that had gathered in his beard. He brushed the bits of his meal from his chin and jacket. "Yeah, yeah. Don't have to yell. I'm here."

"Are there any weapons on your coach? I've got my six-shooters, but that would be like trying to take down a buffalo with a kind word."

"I got a scattergun strapped under the driver's seat."

"I think it's time to get it."

Chester nodded, set his plate down and got up to retrieve the shotgun. He hesitated at the edge of the light, not wanting to walk into the maw of the beast possibly lurking around the corner. He closed his eyes, breathed in slow and long, exhaled out and shook the tingle from his fingers. He opened his eyes and scurried away to grab the shotgun from the front of the wagon.

Levi went to Juliette as she tended to Mary. Mary was coming around but was still dazed after watching her love dragged away.

Juliette looked up. "Where's Chester?"

"He's just grabbing his rifle." Levi picked up some branches and tossed them onto the fire. "It might get a bit hot for a while, but I don't want to get snuck up on again." The wood caught and the flames rose.

Mary came to, disturbed by the burst of sparks as the gambler stoked the fire. "What's going on? Where's Jameson?" Then she remembered what had happened to her husband as Chester rejoined them. Juliette pulled her close and let her weep on her shoulder.

"Found my boomstick, but I only have about six shells, plus the two that are loaded in there already."

"You best wait till you got a clean shot then," Levi said.

He turned to say something to Juliette, but was startled by a rustling just beyond the light of the fire. He drew one of his pistols, his aim settled on his hip to steady the shot. His free hand hovered above the hammer, ready to drop his palm down for a quick succession of shots.

"What is it?" Juliette asked.

"Not sure. Can you maybe hush that woman up a bit so I can hear?"

Juliette nodded and pressed Mary's sobs into her shoulder.

Levi stood motionless. Chester drew up next to him, cocking his shotgun. "You see anything?"

"Not sure," Levi whispered. Thought that I saw—"

He was silenced by the smack of a disembodied arm hurtling into his face, knocking him backward. He hit the ground, and his head glanced on a stone at the edge of the fire ring. The gambler's world went dark.

Chester spun and watched Levi hit the ground. The iron grip of the monster wrapped around Chester's ankle. He yelped as the creature's grip compressed his flesh into a pulp, crushing his bones and twisting his ankle into an unnatural angle. The animal yanked and Chester fell to the ground on his face. Dust plumed around him. The shotgun fell from his grip and out of reach. Panic took hold of him as he stared into Juliette's and Mary's terror-stricken eyes. All three of them screamed in strident harmony as Chester was dragged away into the dark.

Mary, still screaming, broke free of Juliette and spun wildly running toward the dark to escape the horror of the old man's screams. She ran headlong into the roof of the upended stage coach and fell to the ground, out cold.

Juliette stood helpless, looking at her two unconscious companions as the beast feasted on Chester somewhere behind her.

She knelt by Mary. She found a canteen, opened it, and poured a healthy splash of tepid water on the woman's face. Mary spat the water and frantically shook her head. Confusion filled her eyes, but she calmed enough for Juliette to talk.

"I need to check on Levi and I can't do that if you're hysterical. Now hold it together for a minute."

"I—I can hold it together." Mary bit down on her lip.

Juliette got up and moved to Levi. She couldn't tell what had hit him. It had flown out of the dark too fast to register. But as she edged closer, the shape lying next to his head came into view. Glistening in the dancing light of the fire, was Jameson's blood-splattered arm.

Juliette slapped her hands to her mouth, holding back the bile that fought to escape her throat. She had held it together until now. She stumbled over one of the bags they had been sitting on.

She fought with her petticoats and finally righted herself. Levi groaned and pulled himself gingerly to a sitting position. He rubbed his throbbing jaw.

He looked down and started at the sight of the disembodied limb lying next to him. "What the hell?" He kicked it into the dark.

"Where's Chester?" he asked. Juliette pointed a shaking finger at the bloody trail snaking into the dark.

"Jesus," Levi said.

Mary chimed in from where she sat. "He's dead. Dead and

damned and we're next! There's nothing we can do! The devil is out there, and he wants to take our souls like he did Jameson and Chester!" She shook and cried, spitting out the words as Levi held Juliette.

But she was lost. At least in this moment, she was almost beyond being able to consider a world where monsters didn't exist. She had seen the glint of its red eyes, and Jameson's blood, still warm and slick on the teeth of the beast that lived beyond the light of the fire. It had picked off the two men and now there was only the three of them left in the dying light of the flames.

Levi calculated the number of hours before the dawn would chase the fright of night away. He was not optimistic as he looked down at the scant fuel that remained for the fire. He didn't know what else to do.

Juliette wiped away her tears. "I'm okay. Sorry about that." She gently pulled away.

"You sure? Well, this is not going to help us." He motioned to Mary as the woman's panic ramped up again.

Juliette nodded and bent down to pick up Chester's shotgun. She walked over to Mary and held out the weapon. "You want to sit here and feel sorry for yourself until you get ripped away into the dark, too, or are you ready to send that beast back to hell in pieces?"

Mary straightened and scowled. She grabbed the shotgun, looked it over, then stood and wiped away the streaks from her cheeks. "I'm ready to make that thing pay for taking my Jameson away."

The three of them nodded agreement. "Alright then," Levi said. "Juliette, you don't happen to have a weapon, do ya?"

"I doubt anything I have is of much use, but I'll take a look."

She walked over to the ornate case she had recovered earlier. She opened it and looked for anything that could be useful. The silver vanity set glinted in the firelight. At the time that her late husband had presented the gift to her, she thought it vain. Now that he was gone and she found herself on the wrong end of the food chain, she was now for some reason drawn to the elongated handle of the mirror.

The set was solid silver. An heirloom from her dead husband's grandmother. The intricate carvings that adorned the mirror wove around the long handle and ended in a dangerously sharp point. She thought for a moment just how useless this would be, unless an attacker got close and she could stab them—but in this case, the attacker was so large and fast that if it got that close, her weapon would be useless. She stood and left the case open, turned to Levi, and shook her head.

"That's okay." He walked to her and handed her his spare six-shooter. "Just pull the hammer back and squeeze the trigger till the loud bangs stop." He gave a wry smile as she took the gun.

"Until it goes click." She smiled back.

Levi's ears pricked at the sounds just beyond the firelight. A syncopated crackle and crunch rattled gently in his ears. The noise was about a hundred feet away. He squinted into the black, trying to make out what the creature was up to.

Memories of his childhood rolled back to the front of his mind.

When he was a child, his family had a dog. On nights when they were blessed with a bountiful slaughter, his mother would cheerfully share their good fortune with the loyal mutt, leaning down from her cutting board with a bone, freshly stripped from the roast. Saliva would drip from the eager animal's mouth as it panted and patiently waited for the treat to be set in front of it. It would pluck up the moist bone and retreat to its corner of the kitchen to hungrily gnaw at it. While the family quietly dined by the firelight, their dog would scrape, crack, and crunch on its bone, working it back and forth between its jaws, stripping it of its nutrients and lapping at the rich flakes of marrow.

The difference now, was that instead of a prized cow, the beast in the dark was retrieving the marrow from Chester's crooked old bones, hungrily gnashing its teeth across his torn flesh along with that of their other travel companion.

4

The three huddled around the fire. Levi stoked it with scavenged materials from the coach. Mary sat, her knees pulled close, rocking gently to the sounds of her own manic humming. Juliette was next to her, one hand on Mary's shoulder and the other cradling Levi's six-shooter in her lap.

The sounds of feasting had stopped. This bothered Levi. He couldn't tell where the wolf had gone or even if it was on the move. At least when it was sloshing up Chester, they could hear where it lurked beyond the light.

The rush of adrenaline from the attacks ebbed and the chill of the late hour wrapped around them. Levi felt the warmth of the fire and the lull of exhaustion gently tug at his eyelids.

With every weary nod, he jarred himself back to consciousness. He stood up and paced to get his blood moving.

"What do you think it is?" Juliette asked.

"Well, I ain't right sure." He turned on his heels to face her across the fire. "It looks a bit like a wolf, but it doesn't move like one and it sure as hell ain't the size of one."

He squatted and picked up a small stick to prod the fire.

"It's the devil," Mary said. Her voice was thin and child-like. She continued to cradle her knees and gently rock, her eyes wide and unblinking.

"Well, it ain't my barber, that's for sure." Levi chucked a thin stick into the flames and stood.

"Where do you think it is?" Juliette asked.

He turned his back to the fire and stared into the quiet night air. He looked for the animal's movements against the inky backdrop of hilly desert terrain. "I don't know. But I get the feeling it's still hungry."

He turned back to the two women. He sat next to Juliette on the traveling chest that held Jameson's and Mary's clothes. Had she been in a clearer state of mind, Mary never would have stood for such a social slight as to have a strange couple's bottoms plastered on her property. But she was in no place to argue.

The hypnotic pops of the fire and the warmth from its flames ushered the trio into a gentle sleep, their exhaustion getting the better of them.

Juliette started awake. She was roused by the scuff of heavy paws, padding closer to the fire circle. She stayed still, following the sounds with her eyes, squinting into the dark. Her hand tightened around the grip of the pistol nestled in her lap.

She could feel the creature was close, slinking just beyond the glow of the flames. The wind gently shifted, stoking the flames, and pushing the firelight toward the sounds. Juliette made out the silhouette of its spiky rounded shape. It was immense. A head that rivaled the size of the chest they were sitting on. It paced on all fours, its hulking shoulders hunched forward. The matted spikes of fur shook with each step.

Juliette nudged Levi. "I see it," he whispered. He was playing possum like she was. The two of them watched the menacing beast stalk closer to the makeshift campsite.

Then it stopped. The firelight reflected in its onyx eyes. The beast snarled, revealing the massive fangs, tinted pink from feeding.

"Shoot it!" Levi yelled. He leapt up, the hammer already primed on his six-shooter, and aimed at the dark mass just below the wolf's drooling snarl. The first shot whizzed past the wolf's shoulder. The gambler followed the animal's shape as it stretched tall. That it could walk like a man surprised him. Raised up on its haunches, it stretched its neck long and snout to the sky as it released a deafening howl. The sound rattled their ears.

Levi strained to keep focus on his target. He leveled his gun center mass and squeezed the trigger. Two shots rang out. The bullets hit the animal. Its rib cage cracked as they tore through its flesh. The animal's howl was interrupted as it yipped in pain. It dropped to all fours again and teetered back and forth, shaken by its freshly opened wounds.

When the first shot cracked, Mary was ripped from her uneasy slumber. Her eyes went wide as the towering creature filled her vision. She screamed, her vocal cords competing with the stridence of the wolf's howl.

"Juliette," Levi yelled over her shrill cries, trying to snap Juliette out of her frozen state. She turned her attention to him. "Pull the fucking trigger already!" His order was accented by the crack of more shots from his own pistol.

Juliette was in shock. She watched the bullets hit their mark. She heard the thud of their impact as the projectiles ripped through the wolf's body. At that close range, her logical brain told her the animal should be dead. Instead, she watched with horror as the fresh wounds appeared to heal almost as quickly as they had been raised by the bullets. This was brought home by the sound of the bullets hitting the ground as they were pushed out of the wolf's body. Levi's words finally registered in her head. She raised her gun to shoot as the beast made its move.

It lunged for Mary. The air was filled with Levi's gunshots and Mary's echoing screams. The beast grabbed Mary and lifted her in the air. She flailed her arms and kicked her legs as the beast's claws drove into her flesh, piercing through the fine linen of her dress. She was close enough to smell the remnants of her traveling companions and her husband on the wolf's breath. It looked into her eyes, a wicked grin stretching across its glistening fangs. Its nose crinkled in a chuffed snarl.

Mary's screams continued as the wolf lapped its thick tongue up her cheek, sampling its next course. He pulled the screaming woman close, opening its wide maw and nestling her head in between its jaws. The animal brought its heavy jaws down on either side of her skull. Her screams were replaced with the crunch of her skull caving in, bringing her horror to an end. The fanged vice held tight as the animal yanked its muscled arms outward, ripping Mary's lifeless body to twitching hunks of silk-clad breakfast. The splash of intestines at its feet was echoed by the simultaneous click of Juliette running out of bullets and Levi sliding fresh rounds of ammo into his pistol.

The wolf spat the mush of Mary's head from its mouth. The fire hissed as the wet mass plopped into the blaze. A cloud of sparks rose into the lightening early morning sky.

"Get outta there!" Levi yelled at Juliette. She was the closest to the beast now and sure to be its next snack. He leveled his gun higher this time since the body shots had proven less than effective. He sighted on the animal's head and pulled the trigger.

The creature roared as its right ear was blown off. It shook its head and tossed what was left of Mary's body away. It glared at the Gambler and leapt over the fire at him. It landed on Levi and the two went tumbling off to the side. Levi's lungs emptied as the weight of the beast pressed down on him. His bones cracked.

Juliette dropped her gun and picked up a smoldering branch from the fire. She walked to the beast as it continued its assault. She raised the torch above her head and swung for home. The blow started the beast from its frenzy. It turned its attention to Juliette and swatted her away, launching her over the fire into the dark.

Levi now motionless, the creature turned its attention toward Juliette.

She was on her belly, pulling herself along, crawling mindlessly toward any avenue of escape. There had to be a weapon, anything that could hurt the creature that loomed over her.

To taunt her, it raised up one leg and set it down on her left thigh. Juliette whimpered as the animal pressed down and extended a claw into her flesh. Her whimper rose to a scream. She felt the warm drip of saliva on the back of her neck. The beast was bending toward her, sniffing her hair, taking in her scent.

Juliette cried as she continued her desperate search for a weapon. Her hand fell upon the rough etchings of her silver mirror.

The wolf let loose with its hind leg and spun his prey over onto her back. Juliette swung her mirror at the creature's head. Glass shattered and pierced its left eye. The animal's flesh sizzled as the silver connected with its skin. The beast reared back and roared in pain. Juliette kept swinging. Its flesh burned with every strike.

It attempted to strike the mirror from her hand, but she fended off each swipe with a searing connection of the silver to its body. Blisters rose beneath its fur with every strike.

The animal was getting frustrated at the game. It did not like the playmate it was left with. It chomped at the air and swiped its clawed hands at her. But the pain from the mirror was something it had not experienced before. It had had enough. Pain or no, she would be its meal.

The wolf reared up and launched forward. Juliette held her weapon toward it. The animal flew forward, open-mouthed, waiting to accept Juliette's death into his belly as the final offering from the stagecoach. Juliette lunged forward, too. She was sure she would die, but she was not going to let her death be a satisfying kill. She shoved the mirror forward into the mouth of the beast. She felt the pointed end of the handle lodge in the roof of the animal's mouth, the head of the mirror positioned against its bottom jaw. The wolf chomped down, severing her hand from her body. As it closed its jaws, the mirror pressed through the roof of its mouth. The silver sizzled as it ate away at the creature from the inside and pierced its brain.

Juliette watched as the creature went stiff, then fell to the side next to the fire. As she watched the animal twitch the last of its life away, she whimpered and clutched the gushing stump that used to be her hand. She tore at the hem of her dress, pulling free a tattered bandage. She screamed as she tied the fabric around her wound.

She sat there bleeding and watching in horror as the beast that had terrorized them through the night morphed from the towering creature into a naked and bloody man. His bones and cartilage popped as the transformation proceeded. His arms deflated from the furry, muscled weapons they had been, to the freckled and lanky arms of a mere man. She winced at the sight of his head being pushed apart as it shrunk and the mirror that was lodged inside, was pressed further in, the pointed end of the handle jutted out through the eye, while the round body dislocated the dead man's jaw on its journey through the bottom of his jawbone.

Juliette cried at the pain and the loss that the night had brought. She was sure she would die from blood loss. She wondered if the boy who went for help last night had made it to the town or been another victim of the beast. She cried at how tired she was, the adrenaline leaching out from her body as shock set in and the morning chill made her shudder.

"I'll just lay here for a bit and watch the sunrise," she said to herself. She got up and staggered to a boulder. She sat and winced at the sharp twang of pain from her missing hand. She cradled her wound and watched as the sky warmed with the first glow of dawn edging over the horizon. As the sun rose, she slowly slid down the front of the boulder. She settled on the rough ground, propped up by the rock, taking in the warmth of the coming day. She let her eyelids, heavy with fatigue, shield her bloodshot eyes. Soon she tumbled into a deep sleep.

5

Juliette woke as she was jostled and lifted into the back of a wagon. She could just make out two men looming over her.

"What the hell happened?" A gruff voice asked through what sounded like a mouthful of chaw.

"No clue," Jimmy's familiar voice said. "We lost a wheel, and I went to town."

"Well, whatever happened, this little lady is lucky to be alive."

Her eyes adjusted, Juliette could now make out the young stagecoach driver and a man she had never seen before busying themselves around the stagecoach.

"Jesus," the other man said. "Is that a *head?*" The words had barely escaped his lips as he wretched his breakfast onto the ground.

Jimmy jumped up on the wagon. "Whatever happened, she's in rough shape. We need to get her back to town."

The other man nodded spitting the last of the sick from his mouth. He wiped the string of spittle from his chin and joined Jimmy in the wagon.

Juliette passed in and out of consciousness during the ride. Distorted visions of her fallen companions winked at her from the macabre recess of her nightmares. Pain shot through her with every bounce of the wagon as the men rushed her back to town.

They made quick time and delivered Juliette to the town doctor.

Losing her hand in the middle of nowhere should have done her in—but it had clotted enough for her to stay alive until the doctor could cauterize the wound.

Over the next month, Juliette was plagued with the horrible visions that were burned into her thoughts from that night. As the nights wore on, the visions became more visceral. She also noticed sharp pains in her forearm where her hand used to be. She chalked it up to living through a traumatic event and she had heard stories of folks having "phantom sensations" when they lost a limb.

Along with the nightmares came a new craving. She had never been much of a meat eater; but since she had come back from that night, she had near insatiable cravings for the flesh of animals.

After the first days of her recovery, she moved into a boarding house on the outskirts of town. Within a few weeks she was up and about regularly and even started to help with some light chores. But soon she felt that it was time to move on. That, for some reason, there was danger and that she didn't want to bring that danger to the nice people who had taken her in.

She made her goodbyes and booked a ticket for the West. The next stagecoach was scheduled to leave at dusk and arrive at their destination the next morning.

6

The sun had been up for several hours when the lone figure appeared over the rise at the edge of Dry Bed. The woman was dressed in a dark dress, tattered at the edges, and her hair was a tousled mess. She had only a single bag that bounced against her thigh as she walk.

She made a direct line for the saloon and hotel near the center of town. The thud of her heels on the wood planks resounded as she strode into the bar. The smell of last night's cigar smoke and stale beer hung in the air. Behind the bar, a scar-faced bartender gathered dirty glasses in a bin.

"How can I help ya, ma'am?" He said as she came up to him.

"You got any rooms?"

"Got a couple up for grabs. How long you planning to stay?"

"Not sure yet."

"Well, then. It's a dollar a night, or six-fifty a week. Seven if ya want laundry service."

"That sounds fair." The woman fished a hundred dollar note from her bag and set it on the counter. "How about we start with that, and you let me know when my credit is up? That sound good, Mister... I didn't catch your name."

"I didn't give it." The bartender smiled. "Name's Hank. No Mister. And yeah, I can work with this." He pulled a guest book, pen, and key from beneath the counter. "You can have number five. If you wouldn't mind, I need to keep track of my guests. What's your name?"

"Juliette Lupine." The woman pulled a lace glove off her right hand. A faint red scar was etched around her wrist. She smiled at Hank and signed her name in the book.

The Bounty Hunter: Ashe Quaid

7

Ashe saw many things as a bounty hunter.

He saw a Wendigo melt into the sand.

A Chupacabra down near Juarez.

A witch conjure life from the dead.

A preacher strip the life from his entire congregation with a single word.

He used these stories to craft tales when sitting with a lady or at the poker table, but mostly they helped him explain away the things that didn't make sense or that the brain manifested when he had been on the trail too long. They also helped with his reputation, and in his line of work, reputation was everything.

He was on the trail of a fat bounty. A bounty that would keep his belly full and flask topped up with the best hooch for at least a couple of months. No chance he was going to pass up an opportunity like that.

It was ten days since he had seen civilization, such as it was in these parts. Every day he'd find the remnants of a camp site. Each time the same signs. A wet sticky mound of used-up chaw, a dying fire that smelled of weak coffee and burnt beans, and a patch of dirt in the shape of a blanket rolled away in a hurry.

Ashe could have caught up to him already, but he wasn't interested in dragging a body through the desert and dead land if he didn't have to. No sense in stinking up his ride with a rotting corpse when he could follow the trail to the next town and take him out there and get paid by the local authorities. That was exactly where the signs were pointing, and Ashe was in no rush if they were going to be that close to a sheriff's office.

Ashe surveyed the familiar markings of the abandoned camp site. The scene was laid out just like before. Gotta love a creature of habit, he thought. He climbed a boulder to survey the landscape below. The target was consistent when picking camps. Always on elevated ground. Generally, some sort of natural shelter. This time it was the boulder with a leafy tree hanging over it. Just enough cover to stave off a light rain should it rise.

He pulled out a spyglass and smiled. He'd been holding out for a town, and that is exactly where they were going. The rough spires and flat tops of buildings jutted out from the earth just a few miles on. He studied the small town. Gentle plumes of dust from the morning activities mixed with the soft smoke from the chimneys. He could almost smell the bacon on the fire as the town woke and bustled. It was not a big city, but large enough to host what looked to be a good-sized saloon, a general store, a couple of boarding houses, and the usual necessities that allowed a town to function in a civilized manner. There also seemed to be signs of incoming prosperity in the distance. The first elements of an incoming train line were on a crash course to corrupt the quaint hamlet below. Assuming it had not been corrupted already.

Ashe clicked the spyglass shut and stood. He dusted off his chaps hoping there was a laundry in town. So many days out and his eyes were beginning to water when the wind would slow enough for his stink to gather. What he wouldn't give to have a clean shirt, not to mention a bath. His main concern was that the sheriff would have enough cash on hand to clear out this bounty in full so he could rent a room, get a bath, and maybe acquire some female companionship.

He climbed down off the rock and mounted up to head into town. It was only a few miles away. His jaw tensed and mouth watered in anticipation of the sour taste of whiskey soon to be nipping at his taste buds.

Ashe was capable. He had built a reputation for his ability to track, shoot, and how to lay a man down if need be. His current bounty was a real nasty piece of work. He didn't generally get to know his prey too closely, but being on this trail for so long, he'd familiarized himself thoroughly with the list of grievances that coated the bottom of the wanted page and bled onto half the back of the crinkled paper.

> Fred Deckard: 5′ 6″ tall. About 155 lbs. He has dark hair and favors the use of a twin six-gun rig. He is often seen wearing a weathered dark brown bowler. Deckard has been tried and convicted of crimes in Utah, Nevada, New Mexico, California, Texas, and Louisiana. He recently eluded authorities after an escape from a New Mexico constable and is currently on the lam. His crimes include the murder of at least 12 men and women, the unlawful killing of livestock, horse rustling, the robberies of stagecoaches, trains, and banks, assault, rape.

Ashe made good time down the hillside and onto the flat that led into town. It was closer than he had initially thought. He could already hear the rumble of activity and smell the morning offerings from the local boarding houses mixed with the stench of the collection of outhouses throughout the town. The familiar notes of advanced society on the wind were welcome, even with the less pleasant scents mixed in. Such was the way. The good always mixed with the bad. In his experience, no one is clean, and everyone tries to say they deserve a second chance. He was prepared for Fred to plead his case, or try to run, or both. Ashe had little appetite for rogues like Fred. No respect for polite society, choosing to feed his savage tendencies until someone like Ashe stepped in and brought them to justice.

His legs were ready for a break. He was no stranger to the aches of the trail, but after a while, the numbness takes on a pain of its own in the saddle. He was looking forward to a few days off to rest. With the bad came the good and he was ready to sample the town's offerings.

His horse chuffed as the realization of having Ashe off its back for a bit set in. He was ready for a rest as well and Ashe was sure the local stable hands would take good care of him with a little extra coin in their hand.

"There, there, big guy. We're almost there." He gave a reassuring pat to the horse's neck and stroked the outer layer of dust from its mane. "You'll get me off your back soon enough." The horse answered with a gentle quickening of its pace as the jagged horizon of the town came into focus.

Deckard was not considered to be a smart man. He was, however, determined and resourceful enough to keep out of reach for as long as he had. Based on what Ashe had witnessed, Fred would make his way to the whorehouse and saloon to sample the local flesh. That made Ashe's job easy as he narrowed down his options for where to search. He'd ask around to see if someone fit Deckard's description.

As he crossed the town's perimeter there was an archway stretched out above the horse-trodden path. A splintered board stretched between two heavy posts. It read, "Dry Bed. Population 367." The population had recently changed. As was evidenced by the paint from the 7 being bright white while the other letters and numbers were faded. It didn't matter much to him whether it was a loss or a gain, but he remembered a mound of fresh dirt in the town's graveyard to the south that didn't have a marker. The town appeared to be no stranger to the less savory types given its size. That was a good sign. Most sheriffs in these towns wanted little hassle and would generally work with Ashe when taking down his bounty. That way they didn't have to scuff up their boots or disturb their day-drinking other than to telegraph the closest magistrate to advise that a bounty was fulfilled or that a court date for a hanging was necessary.

Everything was familiar in its newness. Ashe took note of the location of the town's livery. He'd circle back there once his business was settled. He tipped his hat to the blacksmith who looked up to inspect the passersby as he hammered away at a glowing piece of iron. There was a post office and next to that a rather good-sized mercantile. A few other businesses appeared to have their eye on the future, being that the railroad was only months away from finalizing work and bringing in more workers, goods, and commerce. There was also a laundry that seemed less than busy but one day would be, along with a tailor, and of course, the sheriff's office.

He would pay the good sheriff a visit as soon as he'd found lodging and a drink of whiskey. Ashe continued to the saloon. He preferred the lodgings of a good saloon to those of a boarding house. There were fewer questions to answer, and fewer prying eyes should he find himself in the company of a lady while in town.

His travels had taken him to several saloons over the years. He'd developed a kind of sense about them. Ashe was not in the habit of looking down his nose at any such establishment, but there certainly was a wide range of quality one could expect from town to town. In front of him rose a sturdy sign.

"Hank's" greeted him with all the welcome he could ask for from a local watering hole. He smiled. He could smell the sin from five hundred yards. He hadn't even tied up his ride and his mouth watered for the sweet taste of whiskey and the salty tang of willing flesh that awaited once he crossed the threshold.

"Hank's" welcomed Ashe as he pushed through the swinging doors and set foot on the weathered floorboards. The space was well lit and full of tables. To the right was a friendly card game. To the left, a lonely cowhand negotiating in whispered tones for twenty minutes of attention from one of the ladies. It was early in the day, so there wasn't much traffic yet.

He had been to saloons that were little more than outhouses serving moonshine, to the nicer establishments that cared what went on in the rooms upstairs. Ashe preferred the latter as he was at least less likely to walk away with a rash or go blind from the booze in a more discerning establishment.

"Hank's" appeared to fall into the latter category and his weary bones were ready for a whiskey, a bath, and the soft touch of a hard woman.

Ashe strolled to the bar and set his saddlebags down. He leaned into the cold marble of the bar top and waived over the scar-faced man behind the counter.

"What'll ya have, stranger?" Hank asked.

"You got any rooms for rent, by chance?"

"Got a couple. Is it just you or anybody joining ya?"

"If I'm lucky I won't be lonely for long, but for decorum's sake, Its just me."

"No need for decorum here." Hank gave what should have been a wink with one of his eyes. "Rooms are a buck a night."

Ashe pulled his billfold from his jacket and laid five dollars on the counter. "How 'bout two nights and a bottle of whiskey to start?"

"Can do." Hank swept the money from the counter and left behind a glass and a freshly corked bottle of whiskey.

"What name should I put on the books, friend?"

"Name's Quaid. Ashe Quaid."

"What brings you to our town, Mr. Quaid?"

"You can call me Ashe. Looking for a man." He plucked the cork from the bottle with his teeth and filled the glass to the brim. He spit the cork into his hand and pressed it back in place.

"Well, I know most who pass through. Is this a good man or a bad man?"

"I suppose it depends on who you ask." Ashe breathed in the sweet scent of corn and grains and took a sip. The sharp sting of homemade whiskey heated his cheeks. He held in the vapors, then let them out with a sigh.

"Well, I'm asking *you,* I guess."

Ashe pulled the warrant from his jacket pocket. He set it down and slid it toward Hank.

Hank picked up the paper and held it up to his good eye. He examined the sketched portrait and took a moment to go through the extensive list of dalliances Deckard was accused of. Once he got to the bounty, a ragged whistle hissed past his crooked lips. He slid the paper back to Ashe. "So not a good man."

"Not for me to judge. Just for me to bring in, one way or another." Ashe took another sip and drained his whiskey. He readied the bottle and glass to pour another round. "I'm guessing from the size of your town you have a law man, is that correct?"

"It is."

"Would you reckon I should talk to him before or after I handle business?"

"I don't follow."

"Some prefer to handle their town's business themselves. Others understand that when a professional is called in, it's best to let them do their work."

Hank thought for a moment. "Sherriff Daltrey is a good man."

"That's good to hear. You know where I might find this good man so I can let him know I'm in town on business?"

Hank swabbed a glass as he thought. "You should probably just head over to his office. He tends to spend much of his day there unless something is going on in town."

"Much obliged. I'd like to freshen up, which way to my room?"

"Head upstairs and to the left. I put you right next to two of our best girls, so be polite."

"I always am, my friend."

Ashe finished his second shot, plucked up the bottle and glass in one hand and his saddle bags in the other, and headed upstairs.

8

The room was clean and comfortable. Ashe set his saddlebags and duster on a chair and closed the door. The bedside table rocked gently as he placed the bottle of whiskey and glass on it. He freshened up at the wash basin. He splashed the layer of trail off his face and neck. As he dried his face, he walked around the room and took in his new lodgings. The room was furnished with a nice-sized bed and a couple of chairs on either side of the clawfoot tub next to the window. He opened the curtains. There was a landing just outside the window should he need a quick escape into the bustling street below. He rebuttoned his shirt, replaced his weathered hat, and headed downstairs to track down the sheriff.

Ashe wasn't a single step out the door when he heard it. Fred Deckard's falsetto laugh was legendary. Ashe had chosen the same establishment as Deckard to take refuge. The harsh cackle erupted from downstairs, followed by the slurpy splat of chaw arcing into a spittoon.

He made his way down the stairs and hailed Hank at the bar.

"Room okay?"

"It is. I'm gonna have to apologize for the mess, though."

"What mess is that?"

Ashe held up a finger, then lowered his hand to rest on the pearl handle of his revolver. He turned to face the braying mule sweating all over his deck of cards like a whore in August. "Fred Deckard!"

Fred bristled at the sound of his name. The room went silent except for his grating laugh trailing off.

"Don't believe I know you, mister. Pretty sure I don't wanna, either." Fred sneered over his fanned-out hand.

"Son, don't make this difficult."

"I ain't yer son, old man." His bottom lip bulged outward, misshapen by the mound of tucked-away chaw.

"And I ain't an old man. Now we can do this easy and let everyone get back to enjoying their drinks or—"

"Or what?" Fred scowled at Ashe.

"Or we do it the less than easy way."

"And who's it less than easy for?"

"For you." Ashe stepped forward.

"You hear this chicken shit, boys? Thinks he's gonna bag him a big bad man today." Nervous chuckles circled the table of card players.

Ashe stopped with two tables between him and his bounty. His best advantage was that Fred was still seated. He flicked the leather strap that secured his gun in his holster.

"Never said I was bringing in a big man. Hell, to call you a man you'd have to have done something manly. All I seen on your warrant are a series of childish outbursts, schoolboy pranks, and acts of cowardice."

"Keep talkin' mister and you'll see just how big I am."

"Big for stealing the poor box from St. Regis? Big for pushin' your 60-year-old nana down a flight of stairs? Big for sleepin' with your ten-year-old cousin?"

"I never touched Enid."

"I'm talkin' about Timmy, ya no good pederast."

Two barstools behind Ashe ground on the floor and

clattered as they were kicked over by their occupants. Two cowhands grabbed his arms and held him in place. "I see you been making friends since you rode into town."

"You'd be surprised what a little bit of coin can get you in a place like this."

"Not really." Ashe grinned and watched Deckard's satisfaction droop.

The two men held him tight, but not tight enough. They had neglected to take his hand off his gun. Ashe shifted his knee to the side. He aimed his holstered pistol into the thigh of the man on his right and pulled the trigger. The pop of gun powder was accompanied by the cowhand's yelp. He dropped to the ground holding his bleeding thigh.

Ashe whipped the still hot barrel from its holster and held it to the neck of his other captor. The man's neck hissed, and he cried out grabbing at the bright red flesh. Ashe swung his forearm around and spun, catching the cowhand at the neck and toppled him over his wounded partner.

Fred dropped his cards and leapt up from his chair. Ashe's gun was smoking before his opponent's cleared its holster. Deckard stood in place for a moment while his brain caught up to the stopping of his heart. His body went limp and he fell to the side. He hit the ground and the hammer on his pistol let loose, shooting off his own big toe.

"God-damn-it!" Hank threw his rag onto the bar.

Ashe turned, walked over to the bar and pulled out his wallet. He pulled a couple of ten-dollar notes from the billfold and laid them on the counter. "That's for the mess."

Hank huffed for a second, then called for his bar boy to drag the dead body out and clean the floor before the evening crowd arrived. His other boy was sent out to fetch the doctor and the sheriff to deal with the two injured men and to clear up the mess Ashe had made.

"Your sheriff prefer to deal with things on sight, or should

I head on over there?"

Hank shook his head. "You might as well stay here. You want a drink?"

"Indeed, I do."

9

"I told you—I was serving a warrant."

"That might be, Mr. Quaid, but I don't appreciate strangers comin' into my town and shootin' up our saloon the first chance they get." Jeb was not a man of good humor when someone drops two dimwitted locals and a fugitive in his town.

"I was on my way to come meet you when the opportunity presented itself."

"Opportunity?"

"Yes. The bar was nearly empty. My bounty was right there and unprepared. Had I waited, the bar might have filled up, or he could've gotten word I was here. If anything, you should thank me for taking care of business so discreetly."

"I ain't amused."

"Well, neither am I, but what's done is done. Now I have a legally tendered warrant that I have served within my rights as a ward of the state. I would appreciate it if you would sign off on this and get me paid so we can all sit down and have a civilized drink together."

The sheriff glared at Ashe for a silent minute.

"He's not wrong, Jeb." Hank swabbed out a glass for the coming evening rush.

"I didn't ask your opinion, Hank. And frankly, I'm not sure how much I appreciate you catering to such customers with violent tendencies."

"You ever been in here on a Saturday night after the railway pays their workers?"

"Enough!" Jeb was flustered, but no matter what angle he looked at the situation, he had to agree that the bounty hunter had handled it the best way possible.

"Look, I promise to be no more trouble. After the chase this asshole rode me on, all I want is some time out of the saddle and to get on the road in a week or so."

"How do I know you won't be no trouble?"

"As Hank just said, you never really know about no one, but I give you my word, I have no intention of raising a ruckus while I enjoy your fine town."

"Ah, hell. Hank! Bring us a whiskey. Not the stuff you make. I want a nice bottle." Hank grimaced, but grabbed a bottle of Uncle Nearest. "And charge it to Mr. Quaid's room."

Ashe acquiesced. Hank brought the bottle with three glasses. They sat and drank while Hank's men escorted the two ruffians to the jail, carted Fred's body away so the undertaker could fit him for a coffin, and mopped up the rest of the sticky mess.

10

Ashe was enjoying a friendly game of cards when he saw her. Wild red hair, as if the world were set ablaze. Emerald, green eyes that shone with a spark of mischief. An infectious laugh and zeal for life that he had not seen in many a woman, let alone a bar girl. She caught his eye, and he lost the hand as quickly as he lost himself in her haunting gaze.

He poured himself a whiskey to nurse the lost wages and she sat down next to him.

"Got an extra glass, stranger?"

"I do, but it'll cost ya."

The boys at the table knew who she was and chuckled.

"Don't mind them. They only wish they could have me sit down next to them without them dropping a week's wages for the attention." She smirked at the now quiet peanut gallery. "Name's Ruby. And you are?"

"Almost outta whiskey. How 'bout you come with me away from this sink hole of a card table and share a few sips?"

"Now that's an offer I'm happy to oblige."

They got up and went to the bar for a fresh bottle and a second glass. Ashe had been in town long enough for Hank to understand that the bill always got paid. He had the bottle waiting along with a glass for Ruby.

"How 'bout we find a little more private place to enjoy each other's company?" Ruby asked.

"I could use a little quiet. Hank, you got any cheroots back there?"

"Just got a shipment in today, in fact."

"Let me have a couple of those then."

He handed over a couple of roughly wrapped stogies. Ashe plucked up a few matches and they were off. Ruby took him up to her quarters, right next to his. She had a nice room with plenty of pillows and silk scarves strewn throughout. There was a copper basin tub on the far side and an elaborate changing screen next to it adorned with stockings and a couple of silk robes. She led him to the far side of the room where there was a door out to the balcony.

"After you, fine sir."

"You are a lady and a scholar."

They drank and Ashe smoked, looking out over the light-speckled streets of the little town. The sleepy railroad stop had not had time to cultivate any large buildings or sprawl. It had the basic infrastructure needed to be considered modern, but other than the hub of commerce surrounding the saloon, it was still little more than a way post. Aside from the church and the houses that tended to be just off the main street. But it was lively without being dangerous and had a quaint warmth to the townsfolk.

The night breeze cooled them and carried the gentle wafts of smoke off into the evening sky. Ashe was going to miss the quiet luxury of relaxing once he picked up his new charge in a week.

"You gonna keep those all to yourself?"

"Huh. Don't get much request from the lady folk for a stogie is all."

"Call me a lady again and I'll slap that right outta your

face. Now share and share alike."

He handed over his spare cheroot and Ruby took after it like a pro. One long tug in and she exhaled a perfect circle of smoke in a single puff.

"Are you gonna make me call you Stranger all night or are you gonna give up that name already?" Ruby smirked; a thin trail of smoke leaked out the corner of her mouth.

"You can call me Ashe."

"So, what's a nice boy like you doing in a town like this?"

"Who says I'm a nice boy?"

"I have a nose for these things."

"Wrapped up a bounty a week or so back. Just been taking some time to recoup before I hit the road again."

"I heard about that. Shot him in the back, I hear."

"Gotta git your stories straight, miss. He and his goons jumped me. I was just takin' care of business. Not my fault he was the business. Besides, I only shoot 'em in the back if they ask nice." He gave a wink to Ruby, his cheroot dangling from the corner of his mouth.

She laughed and took a long pull on her cigar chased by a slow sip of whiskey.

"How 'bout you, Ruby. How long you been here?"

"Not long, but longer than some."

Their attention was pulled away from the small talk by a small dust-up below in the street. They watched as the two brawlers were pulled away from each other by their respective parties to go home and sleep it off.

They spent the next hour making conversation about nothing and working their cigars down to sticky nubs.

"Well, the conversation is grand, but are you looking for more than that this evening, cause the hours are getting on," Ruby said, stubbing out her cheroot on the arm of her chair.

"'Fraid if I stay much longer you won't respect me in the morning."

"I don't respect you now so what have you got to lose?"

"Fair."

They flicked their nubs over the edge and chased each other back into her room.

She was a playful woman with a real passion for her work. He'd been around long enough to have been with his share of bar ladies, and that night with Ruby was quite the ride.

They were woken from their postcoital nap by a to-do in the bar. Ashe jumped up, threw on his trousers and grabbed up his gun belt out of habit.

"Come back to bed, slick. It's got nothing to do with us."

"Probably don't. But I'm gonna go see anyway."

Ruby waved him off and rolled over to go back to sleep.

Ashe stood at the railing, his hand on the pearl of his revolver, and peered over the edge.

Ruby

11

Ruby's eyes popped open, wild with rage and pain. She gasped, the searing heat of the fire around her stinging the inside of her mouth. She had not managed to pull her body back together and not being able to move her head around was disconcerting. She was on the verge of panic. She had been hurt before. Even passed for dead on many occasions. But she had not been dispatched with such severity in longer than she could remember.

The thickening smoke stung. She blinked her eyes closed, squeezing tears down her cheek. She needed to concentrate before it enveloped her. She wasn't sure what would happen if she was fully consumed by the blaze, and she didn't want to find out.

She reached into her mind, concentrating on healing. Tendons and muscle tissue reached out from the severed pieces of her body, searching for purchase to her dismembered parts. Her head was the first to come together. She winced, accepting the pain as the tissues mended and reconnected. Relief washed over her. She was able to turn her head and survey her situation as she continued her mending. The pop of bone and cartilage harmonized with the crackle of the fire that hissed around her.

The room was alive with the fiery blaze. Liquor bottles popped and burst from the heat. An oily blanket of smoke plumed around her, swirling through the Braided Pony. The flames feasted on the dry wood. Rafters creaked from the heat as the fire reached deep inside the timbers, consuming the aged wood in a blazing frenzy.

With a few more snaps and pops of cartilage and bone slamming back in place, Ruby was assembled. She couldn't get up yet, though. The shock of being dismembered and blown to hell was still fresh and she was unable to coax her limbs to work.

She felt the prickle of the rising temperature on her skin. Steam rose from the evaporating puddle of blood she spilled during the attack. The smell of roasting flesh tickled her nose.

The strings on the rickety piano under the staircase pinged as the heat weakened their taut fastenings. One after another they snapped, ripping its insides to shreds as the fire disemboweled the smoldering piano.

Ruby massaged her limbs. Her toes tingled as blood circulated again. She felt her body reviving. The pain of rebirth was worse than the brief memory of her dismemberment at the hands of the two vampires and the wounded sheriff. She berated herself for allowing them to beat her, leaving her weakened. But such thoughts were not going to help in her current situation.

She shook her head, pushing her thoughts of defeat from her mind. She wasn't dead yet.

She needed to avoid the front door in case they were out there watching to make sure she was gone for good. She rolled over to her front. She pulled herself across the splintered floor on her elbows. Her legs were still weak. She slowly inched toward the rear exit.

Burning timbers fell from above, riddling her path with embers and smoking rubble. Ruby wove through the growing field of smoldering obstacles. A rafter broke loose. The crack of the breaking wood was her only warning. Ruby rolled to her right. She shrieked as the searing lumber grazed her side, leaving a freshly charred gash. Even as she healed, she incurred new injuries. It was as if the Braided Pony was unwilling to let go of its final inhabitant. It wanted to cremate her along with itself.

Ruby kept moving, her legs feebly aiding in her escape, pushing her forward along with her arms. The splintered floorboards grasped at the fibers of her clothing. She scraped along, inching her way to the cool night air beyond the rear door. The sound of the inferno was deafening. The lumber screamed under the crushing pressure of collapse as the flames hissed and crackled all around.

The blood that slowly coursed through her awakening limbs, fought to replenish quicker than the fresh cuts leaked it out. Ruby willed herself to press on. Every inch was a mile, but she was not willing to let this be her end. She had fought so long to become who she was, and three men were not going to be her downfall.

As Ruby neared the door, she craved the tease of fresh air that crept past her soot-stained nostrils. The coolness gave her hope. She was able to rise to her knees, but still loped like an injured animal. She pulled herself forward. Her palm slapped on the door jamb. She pulled herself upright, steadying on the warming wood of the passageway. Her knees wobbled as she raised up, still leaning on the building for support. She hobbled one step at a time, crossing the threshold as the upper level dropped down in a hail of fiery debris. Ruby was blown forward by the pressure of the fiery implosion. She fell forward into the tight alleyway between the Braided Pony and the laundry house behind it.

She hungrily sucked in the cool air, fighting past the cloud raised by her awkward landing. She coughed out the sticky smoke from her lungs. Her throat rattled from the forceful gusts of wind as she gasped for fresh air.

She ached from rebuilding her body. She ached from coughing. She lay there and cried as she gathered herself, the roar of the fire behind her and the heat wafting over her body, reminding her that she was still in danger.

Ruby lifted herself up onto her wobbly legs. She leaned away from the burning building, bouncing along the wall of the laundry as she made her way to the end of the alley. She hadn't thought about where the townsfolk would be or what would happen if she was discovered outside of her crematorium. She wanted to get free and away from Thrall since she was in no condition to fight.

She edged around the corner, peering to see if she would be discovered. She had chosen the right direction. No one dashing past or even within sight. They must've all be taking in the bonfire from the street on the opposite side of the building. This was her chance.

Ruby hobbled across the street, her tattered dress trailing the last wisps of smoke from the fire and raising a light trail of dust. She reached the support post of an awning and slumped into it. She took a moment to refresh her breath, then kept moving. She ducked in between two buildings and dragged herself along their length. She checked behind her to make sure there were no witnesses and that she was not being followed. She was close to freedom as she neared the corner of the buildings. She scanned both directions as well as her path forward. She was both relieved and concerned about her route out of town. In front of her lay her best option for escape. Only a hundred or so yards of flat earth lay between her and the town's cemetery. Once she reached that, she would at least have some cover as she navigated the hill behind it. She was concerned that she would be seen as she scaled the barren countryside, but she had no other choice.

She couldn't worry about that. She had to survive and the only chance she had was to keep moving. Her legs would carry her but not fast. *Fuck it. You've come this far, now move that ass or go back and lie down on your pyre.*

Ruby pushed herself upright and leaned forward, urging her muscles to carry her on. She limped ahead desperate to stay alive. The ground beckoned for her to lay down and rest for a bit, but she ignored it. Every step came with less effort than the one before. By the time she reached the weathered gravestones, the limp was replaced with an even stride. Every step was filled with determination. She was tired and God knows starving. She would need to rest soon but to rest now would mean another confrontation and she was in no condition to fight. She kept moving, her posture straightening, and the pain becoming less dominant with every stride.

Ruby heard distant yells behind her. She dropped to her knees and huddled behind a large wooden grave marker. She peered around it to see if the voices were following her or just going by. Two figures, masked by the shadows of the buildings, dashed along in search of something. She couldn't be sure if they were looking for her, or perhaps just buckets to carry water to the fire. She watched them as they appeared to find what they were looking for and then disappeared back into the town and away from her.

She waited to be sure then got back up to press on. A faintness came over her and she swayed. She steadied herself with the grave marker. The black spots in her vision dissipated as she blinked them away and got her breath.

"Come on, Ruby. You can't stay here all night. One foot in front of the other," she rasped to herself.

She pinched the bridge of her nose, squinted her eyes, took a cool breath in and breathed out. She opened her eyes. They were still blurry, but the spell had passed, and the world was coming back into focus. She let loose her grip on the marker and started up the hill.

As she crested the hill, she turned to look down on Thrall. She had enjoyed her time there for the most part, but she had also let herself get complacent. She was there for too long and that is what got her in trouble. It always did. Even for a creature such as herself, relationships muddy the water, and she had let her guard down.

Thrall lay below, the flames of the Braided Pony glowing at the center of the small township. The moon shone bright painting the buildings bellow in shades of blue and lighting the world with a gentle white hue.

"Fuck 'em if they can't take a joke." She smirked and turned toward the other side of the hill in search of refuge and hopefully a meal.

12

Ruby needed to feed. Not to survive, since she could survive for years without nourishment. But of course, that was just existing, not living. The longer she went without food, the weaker she would become, and since she had just gone through so much physical trauma, without sustenance she would not be able to fully heal.

She had another dilemma, though. She needed to get as much distance between her and Thrall as she could. To feed meant leaving behind evidence that she was still alive, and she was in no hurry to put her three friends from the Braided Pony back on her tail, especially in her current condition.

Animals were a better option than overtaking a farmstead, but that meant catching one. Again, since she was so weak, her speed would not be accessible the way she was used to. And farm animals, being keen to the smells of danger, would also be hard to approach without scaring them off.

Still, she would have to take some chances.. She walked on, each step becoming more natural, but also bringing her fatigue to the surface.

She had been moving west for a couple hours no farms in sight. No specks of light seeping through windows. No streams of smoke from the dinner fires. She kept scanning and running. She was hoping to make the cover of the surrounding range of mountains by daybreak and put some real distance between her and Thrall. The dark silhouette of the looming crag slowly grew near as she made her way across the rough earth.

The call of a coyote tickled her ear. *Wanna dance, my friend?* She quietly taunted the far-off creature in hopes of coaxing it closer. She doubted its nervous nature would allow it to inspect her close enough to grab a snack. She hoped that the wooded path before her in the mountain would yield better results. She could hunt and eat there without bringing any attention to herself. She could only hope that some bit of strength could be called upon when the time came.

Something caught her attention. A small but sharp sound scratched the earth to her left. She stopped for a moment, letting the quiet of the night wrap around her so she could identify the sound that was out of place. Then she saw it. A foot or two to her left, the moonlight reflected off a coiled shape. She had heard the rough scales scrape across the dirt and now looked down into the dark eyes of a sidewinder winding up to strike.

Ruby stood still. The snake sprang forward. She let it land on her. She winced at the sharp insertion of fangs. The snake's large head clamped down on her calf, instinctively pumping its venom into its prey.

She flexed her muscles, clutching the snake's fangs between the strands of muscle in her leg. She reached down, grabbed the snake just below the head, and gave a quick yank. The head stayed in place, as she ripped the body away from it. The headless body whipped in the air, its motor function contracting its muscles. Ruby raised the body up to her lips and drank from a steady stream of blood and spinal fluid. The warm infusion rushed through her body, and she shivered, the feeling of life coursing through her body.

The rush of food and the injection of venom made her giddy and lightheaded. She giggled at the euphoric wave that washed over her. She swayed gently, enjoying the moment, the remnants of the snake's body dangling from her fingertips.

She looked down at the snake's head, still attached to her calf. She gave a chuckle and plucked it free. The wound healed as the long fangs withdrew. She looked into its dead eyes and gave a playful kiss to its nose. "Thanks for the pick-me-up. Hope it was as good for you as it was for me."

She dropped the head next to the rest of its remains and started for the hills that lay in front of her, her stride a little brisker and feeling better, the snake's flesh already incorporated into her blood stream. The snake's offering kept her going until morning and she was thankful for the encounter, but she needed much more to fully heal.

13

The snake refreshed Ruby considerably for how small it was, illustrating for her, just how hungry and injured she had been. But as much as it helped, its effects subsided quickly. Her strength flagged again as the sky lightened with the coming dawn.

She managed to make the distance and put Thrall well behind her. If the town suspected that she was dead, she would be able to continue forward and to heal. She passed into the trees, leaving behind the desolate plain, entering the mountain landscape.

14

Though she had healed from the snake bite, as she weakened again and the nourishment from the snake ebbed, the wound had reappeared and begun to seep. This worried her as she had not been this weak and injured for a long time. She needed a more substantial meal, or she worried that her injuries from the row at the Braided Pony would begin to take hold again as well. That's all she needed was to find herself falling apart in the middle of nowhere.

She scanned the woods for signs of wildlife or even travelers. A human or two would do the trick, but she was willing to settle for a mountain lion or badger if she could find one. But being so weak, she could not be confident in her ability to successfully hunt anything.

Her ear perked at a familiar sound. Someone was whistling. She was sure it wasn't a bird call. Or at least she hoped not. Unlike a birdcall, the whistle wove through a somewhat familiar melody. She was sure of it. It was a song she remembered. An old song, one that she was sure she had heard on her journeys. Not just her journeys, though. It was from her world, the world before the lust and the feedings. A time that was buried in her past so far, she was sure it would never be unearthed again. But here was her past coming back to lead her to what she hoped would be her salvation.

She walked on, ignoring the seeping wound and the aching body that screamed for rest. The thick woods opened. She found herself at the bank of a gentle stream. The round stones beneath the surface rolled along, carrying the water from the spring it emerged from.

The whistling called her to the stream and then left. She looked around for any sign of its creator. Then it was back. It was upstream. Not near, but close enough for her heightened senses to pick up. Luckily, not everything was failing on her. She followed the sound, letting it soothe her pain and remember a time before.

15

She followed the whistler's warble. The stream broadened into a river that wound through the wooded area, then narrowed the closer it got to the base of the mountain. The tree line receded and the stone embankments grew sharper and more difficult to navigate.

Along with the whistling, she now discerned scraping sounds and the crackling of a campfire. She sensed one person nearby but that would suffice. She moved back to the river for a clearer view.

As she emerged from the tree line, there he was. A prospector panning for nuggets. That explained the scraping sounds. She was relieved that he was on her side of the river and still oblivious to her presence. She had a chance.

Ruby crept nearer, her thirst screaming.

The man swished his pan. Once again, the riverbed delivered no luster. He emptied his pan and bent down to refill the tin with a fresh bit of silt when he saw her. Her feral appearance gave him a start. "Holy hell!" He clutched his chest in astonishment and then gave a chuckle. "You gave me a fright there, miss. Where'd you come from?" She kept silent but kept walking toward him. "Ma'am, are you okay?" He stood, the contents of his pan swishing and wetting his pant leg as it splashed over the side.

Ruby said nothing. Her eyes darkened as her change took hold. She quickened her step. The world was a blur around her. The hunger burned in her gut and her jaws ached to sink into the aged prospector's flesh. She raced down the riverbed, her arms outstretched, mouth wide, and elongated tongue flailing about.

The man was petrified by the wild vision that sped from the trees toward him. He didn't have time to react before Ruby was on him. She launched forward, latching onto him. Her legs wrapped around him. His tin pan dropped with a clatter on the rocky riverbank. His arms flailed as he attempted to fight her off. She tightened around him, her arms and legs constricting, pressing her face into the crook of his neck. He screamed as her wet fangs plunged into his flesh. He fought for his life, hammering away at her back and sides ineffectually. She inhaled the gush of blood that flooded her mouth. Her elongated tongue dove past her teeth and burrowed deep into his body. His knees buckled and the two of them fell to the ground. His desperate screams gave way to a wet gurgle. Aside from the occasional twitch triggered by his dying nervous system, his weakened body stopped struggling beneath her and she loosened her grip.

As she fed, she healed. With a more substantial victim, she was able to replenish herself but the prey being a human, she knew the effects would be temporary. She needed to find a vampire, or her darker nature would eventually emerge without her being able to mask it from the public. But for now, she was sated. She rolled off the prospector's limp corpse. The cool rocks of the riverbank felt refreshing as she stared up at the blue sky. A smile stretched across her blood-stained lips. She exhaled a satisfied sigh and let her eyes close to enjoy a late morning nap.

16

When she woke, Ruby finished stripping the body of its nutrients. Little remained after gorging herself as if it was the first time she had ever fed. Afterward, she removed her tattered, blood-soaked dress and walked into the cold river. She scrubbed away the sticky remnants and freshened up from her sojourn through the forest. She yearned for a hot bath but was refreshed by the nip of the cool river.

The man had been camping out for a while, staking his claim. He had a large canvas tent and a rough kitchen set up. Inside the tent she found his sleeping roll, a lantern, and a wooden chest. She was glad to find clean clothes in the chest. She chose a linen shirt, suspenders, and denim pants. She took the boots and socks off the dead man. The socks she gave a quick soak in the river and hung them over the fire to dry.

She found a pouch with about ten decent sized nuggets. She would trade those in at the next town to get herself some fresh clothes to go along with her fresh start.

Ruby took the remainder of the day and most of the night to rest. She woke to the sound of a family of raccoons scavenging the body of the panhandler. They scurried away too soon to get her morning snack, but she decided it was time to move along.

She gathered up the money and gold nuggets she found, a canteen for water, and the large, brimmed hat. Since her rebirth she had found herself to be more sensitive to the light than usual, so she decided to take precautions. Lastly, she pulled on the dried socks and panhandler's boots and continued her trek through the mountains.

17

Ruby hiked most of the day. Her revitalized senses probed the woods for any possible meal opportunities. As dusk set in she found a hiding place to watch for wildlife. From there she kept watch for animals that wandered close enough for her to pounce. The panhandler would sustain her for a few days, but since she had grown weak, she wanted to keep her energy stores well stocked.

She waited in the brush, more silent than the trees themselves. She disrobed so as not to soak her new duds in blood. She hoped her dip in the river would mask her scent enough to not scare off wildlife.

It didn't take long before she heard rustling off to her left and about fifty yards away. She trained her eyes on the source. It sounded larger than a raccoon—promising. The underbrush parted about ten yards away to reveal a large stag. Judging by its gait, she had not been detected yet.

Ruby crouched, ready to spring into action. She waited for the deer to move forward into the clearing so she wouldn't have any obstacles as she made her move.

The deer cautiously took in its surroundings.

It took a step into the clearing. Ruby pounced on it. Her talons sliced clean through its neck. She clutched the headless torso and drank from the warm salty fountain that spewed forth. She made quick work of the large animal. Two large meals in such close succession did wonders for her. She left the carcass and rinsed off in the nearby river before getting her clothes back on and opting to travel the rest of the night.

Getting to feed allowed her to continue at her quick pace. Using her powers to take down the deer had drained her reserves so that her masking abilities were less than optimal. Her cheekbones took on a more angular shape, as opposed to the soft apple cheeks her customers had grown accustomed to, and her fingers were elongated. From far away she would appear normal, but up close, her features leaned more toward her darker self. Polite society would be less pleased to have such a crone among them if she didn't remedy her feeding situation soon.

18

Ruby continued through the mountain pass for two weeks. She rested during the days, hunted in the evenings, and hiked at night to limit her exposure to the sun. The wildlife sustained her, but her thirst was growing beyond what the forest animals could supply. Of course, she could survive like this for a long time. But she was not interested in surviving. She enjoyed *thriving*.

She looked for smoke. Listened for songs, talking, or livestock. She lived with the knowledge that she had no true idea of where she was, having never been in this part of the West.

A few days after she crested the mountain, she caught site of her first signs of man. To the north, there was a town. It was several days' journey away, but she heartened at the idea of a strong whiskey and the company of a strong man. The other thing she saw was the first sign of a claim at least five or so miles outside the town. If inhabited, she could refuel before town, so she was at least minimally transformed upon her arrival. It appeared secluded enough to visit and supply up before heading down to the rest of the townsfolk. Hopefully the inhabitants would not be missed before she was able to settle in in the town.

It took Ruby a full day to make her way down to the residence. It was a small, stone cottage. She skulked around the perimeter. It had a clearing adjacent to it that was corralled and housed a decent flock of sheep. The bleating animals nervously circled their paddock as she neared the homestead.

There was no sense getting any closer to them. They would just alert the residents of her presence. The main house was a good size for a small family and had a barn with some horses. She avoided the barn for the same reason as the sheep. She stayed out of site until the sun was swept away by the moon. As night rolled in on the wooded valley, Ruby moved in on the house.

19

James and Mary were wedded less than five years ago. James had waited to court the fairer sex until he felt he had made his own way in the world as a rancher. His sheep had turned profitable and then he met Mary. Though there was an age difference, that was common for that time and that area. Mary was married off to James after a courtship was agreed upon and the dowry was paid. It helped that they had a natural appreciation for each other. It also helped that James was not interested in children and that Mary was infertile due to a childhood illness.

James and Mary kept mostly to themselves, spending little time in the town. James did his business with customers on the other side of the mountain, so aside from supply runs in town, they would not be missed for quite some time.

They heard a knock at the door.

"Who could that be?" James asked, a bit concerned as they rarely got visitors, especially this late in the day. But he tended to be a trusting sort.

James rose from his rocker by the fireplace. Mary halted her knitting and watched nervously as James approached the door. He opened it. There was a short man in work clothes facing away from him.

"How can I help ya, stranger?"

Ruby slowly turned. James's eyes bugged out as the grotesque vision of her was revealed. Eyes like darkest onyx bored into him. A mouth that stretched from ear to ear in a devilish grin, filled with daggers, dripping with saliva. Her fingers were thin and elongated with curved talons.

Ruby breathed heavy in anticipation of the kill. Her hat dropped to the ground letting loose her vibrant red locks. Her tendril-like tongue moved like a viper waiting to strike.

James gripped the door and flung it closed. But Ruby stopped it short. Her claws pierced the door, almost driving into James's eyes. James propped himself against the door to hold her out. "Mary, run!"

Mary shrieked as she bolted up, tripping on the blanket she had been knitting and scrambling on the floor to get out the back door.

"I'm just a weary traveler looking for a meal!" Ruby cackled.

James wrestled with the weight of the door. Ruby ripped a handful of timber loose. James's weight pushed the door closed, but Ruby's fist connected with his eye and knocked him to the side.

Mary ran out the back door.

Ruby kicked the door open. The crunch of bone rang through the room. He moaned on the floor as Ruby eyed the back door. "Time to play." She dropped to all fours and launched herself through the door.

Mary wove through the trees. She had no destination. Her path was fueled by fear. She sobbed as she ran, and she was beginning to get short of breath. The sound of Ruby closing in on her motivated her to keep going.

Ruby had shed her boots again. Her toes had sprung short claws, and she ran now more like a canine on the hunt than as a human. Her time in the woods had brought on certain changes. Changes that she had learned to disguise over time, but without a steady infusion of vampire essence or, at the least, human blood, the beast within took hold.

She could have taken Mary at any moment. She preferred to play with her food before indulging in her meal. She let Mary continue until the woman's lungs gave out and there was no more fun in the chase. Ruby lunged forward and landed on Mary, skidding to a halt on the woman's back, her claws planted firmly in Mary's back, piercing her lungs.

Ruby turned Mary over. She leaned down with a hungry grin parting her lips. She devoured Mary's head in a single, slow bite.

The sustenance she gained allowed her to morph back into her publicly accepted beauty. That night, she drew herself a cold bath from the couple's well, warmed slightly by the water on the fire. She scrubbed away weeks of grime that had accumulated while she was in the mountains. The fulfilling meal would allow her a few days to acclimate to the town below, and Mary's clothes would allow her to stop dressing like a prospector, and hopefully make some ins at the local saloon, allowing her to resume her favored activities once again as she regrouped and decided if she was going to try and find her old friend Finn again.

20

Ruby worked fast to establish her place in her new surroundings. Within a few days, she had found a space in the town's cleanest saloon. She worked the room in her plain clothes, gathering the funds to upgrade her attire. Soon the town knew of the new girl with an appetite for her profession and the skills to entertain any and all offers.

Her coffers were replenished, and her lifestyle resurrected along with her hunger.

On nights she felt the pull of the inner beast, she'd avoid the trappings of the saloon and find sustenance on the surrounding farms and even in the rare passer-through. Her ability to blend in and to dispose of evidence of her feedings was made easier by the fact that the town had a rather large hog farm just on the outskirts. Any leftovers from her meals were deposited for the ravenous animals dispose of.

Her only obstacle was the growing popularity of the local preacher. A tall, skeletal man with thin gray hair, a gravelly baritone voice, and a constant smile that stretched his thin lips to their limit across his yellowed teeth. Ruby had gone head-to-head with many a holy man over the years, but this one was different. Even though the other ladies at Hank's told her he tended to sample the new hires so he could piously warn his congregants of their sinning ways, he avoided Ruby. He was unbending in his preachings, and Ruby had a distaste for hypocrisy. Their only fleeting meeting was cold, and they barely exchanged a few words.

There was an air about the preacher that Ruby didn't trust. He was hiding something and that reminded her too much of herself.

21

Hank's resonated with energy. Scouts for the railroad had made their way to town and brought with them money and the appetite to spend it on flesh, booze, and cards. Ruby was beginning to feel her deeper hunger and her outer façade was ebbing. She still had the looks to draw in the wanderers, but she was taking on a more matronly exterior with her sharpened features and strands of gray weaving their way into her hair.

"Look a bit piqued tonight, Ruby. You need to take a spell?" Hank said as he worked the rusted basin water out of a tumbler with his bar towel.

"Stuff it, pretty boy. Just keep my glass full and worry about not scaring off any potential customers, eh?"

"No need to be sour. Just lookin' out for you." Hank put down the glass and filled Ruby's with a healthy pour from his private stock.

"Sorry, hon. Don't mean to take it out on you. Just tired tonight but need some coin." Ruby took a swig from her glass, letting the liquid tickle the inside of her mouth with the sweet and spicy notes of moonshine.

A tingle ran up her spine, but not from the booze. It was a familiar sensation that she had not felt for some time. Her senses went on high alert as she turned to take in the scene of the saloon and find the source of her heightened awareness. Her gaze wove through the room ticking off the unlikely candidates, those that she knew and those that were obviously not what she was sensing. She eliminated one cowhand after the next until only one raised her curiosity.

A man sat alone next to the winding staircase, a half-empty bottle of whiskey keeping him company as he surveyed the crowd. She knew that look. It was not the look of a customer browsing the goods. It was the focused stare of a hunter. His narrow eyes scanning the crowd for the best prey. He sat patiently sipping his drink and waiting. He was hunting for flesh all right, but not in the way most do at Hank's. He was narrowing his selections down, looking for healthy folks that wouldn't be missed. She knew this tactic. Find a newcomer who has made their claims of only passing through, that way, when they disappear, no one raises an eyebrow.

He appeared to have whittled down his options and Ruby needed to be his focus before he made his move elsewhere. She'd lure him in to confirm what she sensed. Confirmation that would allow her to return her strength in full on a more permanent basis. This was her chance to hunt again. And now that she'd identified him, she was sure he was what she needed, a vampire. Only a vampire would replenish her beyond what her usual cattle and vagabonds had. Time for Ruby to live again.

"Who's the stranger?" She asked Hank as she turned back to him, glass empty and awaiting a refill.

"Not sure. Saw him pull in just after dusk. He hasn't asked for a room yet, so I figured he was a railroad scout with his own tent or put up in the boarding house already."

"Well, he looks yummy. I think I might take a bite out of him tonight."

Hank chuckled and shook his head as he filled Ruby's

glass. "Always appreciate your enthusiasm. Best get at it, though. Looks like he has Maria in his sights."

"I'll throw her a coin so she don't feel bad. Besides, she never has trouble filling her bed."

"Just play nice, that's all I ask."

"Nice is in the eye of the beholder, my friend." Ruby jested, pointing at Hank's bad eye.

"Real funny."

Ruby turned back to her prey, slugged back half the glass of whiskey, and rose to make the trek across the room. As she walked, she got Maria's attention to indicate she was making a move. Maria stuck out her lip in a playful pout. Ruby flicked a half-dollar piece to her to pay for her troubles. Maria plucked it from the air, a grin pulled across her face just as one of the gamblers pulled her down laughing onto his lap. Ruby winked at her already preoccupied coworker and continued toward her target.

The vampire maintained his focus on the room. Ruby made sure to insert herself into his view. She leaned over a table of gamblers mid-hand, told them a bawdy joke, her cleavage spilling forward. The men exploded with laughter. She hip-checked one of their shoulders and laughed along while downing the last of her whiskey.

From the corner of her eye, she saw that it worked. The engagement with the card players grabbed his attention and he was focusing his gaze on her. "That's it, honey, come to mama."

Ruby wiped her forearm across her lips to dry the remnants of whiskey, then locked eyes with the vampire. His blue-silver orbs cut through the thick, smoke-filled air like knives from under his wide-brimmed hat.

Ruby noticed an urging sensation, familiar to her as a vampire's influence. A little parlor trick many pick up to lure their prey. He had fallen for it and was reeling her in. Even in her weakened state, his influence had no real affect. But she was able to play the part and wove her way to his quiet table.

"Any way a girl could help a man get to the bottom of that bottle? Maybe even entice him into the bottom of something else along the way?" Ruby gave him a lascivious grin and licked the inside of her empty glass.

"Certainly, wouldn't mind some company tonight and happy to share in my bounty with a potential playmate." The stranger grinned up at her, tipping the brim of his hat up slightly to acknowledge the presence of a lady. "Pull up a chair." He gently kicked out the chair opposite him with his toe.

"Much obliged." She gave a girlish giggle and swung her hips around, seductively setting herself down in the seat in front of him. She pushed her empty vessel his way as he uncorked his whiskey and poured out an ample splash that continued to fill until it hit the brim of her glass.

"Question is, can you kill that without spilling a drop?" He leered.

"Ooh, is that a challenge?" Ruby winked and stared hard at the brimming glass. She acted as if she were going to pick it up, then leaned down, making sure to give a playful glance up at him as she wrapped her lips around the mouth of the glass. She held it tight with her lips sealing the liquid from any spillage. She maintained eye contact with the stranger as she raised up and leaned her head back, draining the entirety of the glass in a single motion. She let loose with her lips and the glass dropped down into her waiting hands. Letting out a gasp, Ruby grinned back at the appreciative gaze of the stranger as she lapped at the single droplet that crept down her chin.

"How's that?" Ruby grinned triumphantly and bowed to the few people who had witnessed her display and were applauding with ruckus glee.

"Impressive." He tipped his hat and raised his own glass in cheers to her feat. He took a slug, then refilled both their glasses.

The two of them joked and flirted for the next hour, both feigning the effects of the alcohol more than what was truly affecting them. After the bottle went dry, he made his move.

* * *

The two stumbled out of the saloon. The creaking doors bade them goodnight. They laughed and clung to each other to stay upright as they tromped down the stairs leading to the street. A couple passed them, tsking their disapproval of their taboo activities visible from the street and shaking their heads as they hurried past. They paid them no heed as they giddily scuttled away.

"Where's your place, handsome?" Ruby slurred dutifully, playing her part.

"Just up here and down the alley."

"Good, I can't wait to get you alone."

He pulled her close. "Why wait?" He whispered with devilish intent.

He guided her quickly to the alleyway behind the saloon. He spun her to face him and kissed her hard. Ruby inhaled his essence. It lit her insides on fire, and she squeezed him, feeling his firmness press between her thighs. They both groaned with acceptance and wrestled to maintain contact.

Ruby pulled away, playfully holding the panting man back. She grabbed his shirt and spun him around slamming his back against the wall of one of the buildings in the thin passageway. "Be patient, lovey. I want to sample all of you before you pop." Ruby licked her lips and smiled at him, a glint of mischief in her eyes.

"Out here?" He looked nervously around. He was not used

to such an aggressive plaything, but he was enthralled by her and was more than willing to partake in his prey before feeding.

"Just lean back." Ruby put a finger to his lips and knelt on the soft ground in front of him. She wasn't lying. She did want to sample the vampire. Their kind knew how to please her, and as hungry as she was, the fire in her loins was taking precedence.

The vampire kept lookout as she undid his pants and began to taste him, controlling the moment, letting him pass in and out of her mouth and lap up the moment before pulling away and bolting up for a wet kiss. The vampire, taking his aggressor's cue, lifted Ruby up, pressing her up against the wall, maneuvering underneath her dress. He ripped away her undergarments, delving his tongue deep between her thighs.

Ruby moaned, letting each wave of ecstasy build while he hungrily lapped at her. "I must have you inside me!" He didn't stop, so Ruby put her raised leg on his shoulder and pushed him off and down onto his back. She dropped down on him and mounted him, letting him slide inside her. They both savored the connection, clasping each other and pressing themselves as close to one another as they could. They writhed in the shadows of the alley, not caring if they were discovered.

Ruby leaned down and kissed him gently, tracing her tongue around the shape of his supple lips. She rode him, driving him deep inside her, slowly at first, letting the tension build as they learned the others' movements and needs. A gentle cloud of dust rose around them as they worked each other into a frenzy. Ruby had not felt this connected physically to someone since Finn. She wanted to savor the moment but felt her hunger rise. She ground away, writhing on top of him, bringing herself to completion just as he tensed up. She let out a loud gasp and a squeal. The vampire, self-conscious about the kill he thought he was about to make, wanted to quiet her. He thrust his hand up to her mouth, stifling the remainder of her orgasm into his hand. She kissed it and licked between his fingers as the waves of pleasure ebbed away.

She felt his other hand grasp her hip and tighten, holding her down. It was time. Ruby let the transformation begin even as he was finishing inside her. Her tongue continued to work his fingers but grew and stretched past them and down his arm quickly securing him as it tightened. He looked up confused at what he was seeing. Her hands, resting on his chest, flexed and her talons sprang forth, puncturing through his shirt and skin, cracking ribs as they grew and curled around his insides.

"What the fuck are you?" He stared up at her transformation in horror.

"The best lay you ever had. But now I'm hungry for round two. Don't go soft on me yet, baby."

Her paralytic took hold, and his strength and powers were useless. She pulled his hand into her elongated maw and chomped down, her eyes rolling back with an extension of her orgasm as the vampire's blood splashed down her throat. She ripped the hand free and let it fall to the ground next to them. He couldn't move. She retracted her claws from his chest and took hold of his other hand and the bloody forearm and pressed them down to the ground on either side of his head.

A single tear leaked down the side of his face. His eyes were frozen open staring up at Ruby. She flung her hair back from her demonic face. He stared up at her smile colored by the blood from his hand. Her onyx eyes reflected his horror back at him as she stared hungrily down at him.

"I can't tell you how much I needed this, lover. Too bad

this won't be as good for you as it is for me." Her Cheshire grin spread as she opened it. Her elongated tentacle of a tongue shot forth and wriggled down his throat. She continued to ride his body to another orgasm as she obliterated his insides with her tongue, lowering her mouth down to drain his liquified insides. She needed every bit of him that she could extract. She fed on him until he was little more than an empty husk. His elastic skin spread across his bones, all meat and organs consumed as she sated her hunger. She pulled back, retracting her tongue, a bloody trail dribbling down her chin. He wasn't moving but he was still a vampire, so she did what was necessary to finish the job. She opened his mouth wide, and extracted his elongated canines with her talons, dropping them into her leather pouch around her neck. She swiped her index finger across his throat, severing his head from his body. It rolled to the side and rocked back and forth for a moment. She rose, extracting herself from him and giggled as the aftershock rolled through her. "Oh, baby, that was one for the books." Back in human form, her hair a buoyant bright red, her skin dewy, and every bit of her feeling like herself again. She gave a thankful yelp to the universe for delivering such a satisfying meal.

She looked around to make sure no one had decided to peep on their little encounter. With the coast clear, she hefted the vampire's body onto one shoulder, plucked up the head in her other hand and crept toward the burn pile that was always incinerating the town's daily refuse. The fire would be lit but at this hour the tenders would be enjoying the simple creature comforts at Hank's.

Ruby stealthily made her way to the burn pile and deposited the vampire's remains.

22

Ruby was a hit with the locals and transient workers, and now that she was back to full power, her confidence was present in every interaction. Even her verbal sparring matches with the preacher and his followers were becoming a satisfying element of her days. She almost felt sorry for them in their ineptitude. The problem was they believed these interactions to be personal attacks and saw her as a threat.

Outside of these interactions, Ruby was at home in her ways. Each day was spent searching the crowds for apt playmates. Sometimes finding a short-term connection, usually just engaging in passing the time with a little carnal back-and-forth.

That is, until the day the bounty hunter walked in. He didn't have the dark aura of her vampire prey, but his ability to dispatch his foes, throw back a drink, and maintain a calm demeanor drew her in. He would be a fun plaything while he was around.

She stood at the top of the stairs and admired his physicality. His fighting was creative yet disciplined. He was strong and quick and moved like a warrior. His clothes, though trail-worn, showed care and appreciation. They were fitted to him and moved with every shift of his body. He was decked out in dark slacks, a cream button-down shirt with no collar, and a dark brown leather vest. His hat was well-trained but maintained its crisp mesa lines.

She watched as he dispatched his prey with ease. Not bad for a human. She waited for the dust to settle and for him to find a rhythm after a while at the saloon. She sauntered down the stairs and locked eyes with him as he wrapped up a hand of cards and reeled him in.

Brother Thomas

23

Wisps of gray and white hair clung to Brother Thomas's head. Perspiration beaded on his nose before diving off to wet the pages of his aged and tattered Bible. He panted; the wind taken from him by his impassioned delivery. His mouth was stretched tight in a wide smile, baring his yellowed crooked teeth. His cream-colored linen shirt clung to his skeletal frame. He lifted his head to address his wide-eyed congregants.

"Brothers and sisters. We all know the trials that the flesh peddlers and sinners of the world continue to taunt and tempt us with." He stood tall and smoothed back the stray hairs that disobeyed their training. The congregants nodded and grumbled their agreement. "How long must we tolerate the whims and the antics of the blind as they allow the fornicators to taint our fine town with their dirty ways?

"Why, just the other day I was speaking to our town's mayor and was disappointed in his inability to see the whores and miscreants who inhabit and fornicate at the saloon for what they are. Demons of the flesh, every one of them. Though it be *God's* and not *my* place to condemn, I would go so far as to say that many of these foolish sinners be beyond redemption."

Complacent nods and grunts of muffled, "Amens", filled the humid room, punctuating each of Brother Thomas's remarks.

"Doesn't this book," His hand slammed down on his podium atop his Bible startling a napping child in the front row, "harken to the dealings of the flesh as if to remind us that unless you are bringing a follower into this world, then you best keep your seed where it be? There should be no slippery escapades for those that believe in the great thereafter. Your rewards come from your devotion to God, not from your bestial yelps as you play at love in your marital bed. And lest ye forget, the marital bed is the *only* acceptable place for you to plant those seeds lest you be cursed with a diseased crop!"

The nods continued, even though many of those in attendance did not abide with such a prudish doctrine when outside the church walls.

The sermon continued and the pastor raged for another hour. Ruby always liked to make sure he saw her walking by when the heat of the day would egg him on to such heights of puritanical frenzy. She'd loudly click her heals on the wooden planks of the stairs that led up to the open doorway and then stand smiling at him. They both knew the hypocritical nature of his flock would have them nodding at his words while later at least some of the congregants would be nodding their heads between her thighs as she preached her own gospel to balance the scales.

Today she stood for just a few minutes since his rants bored her. She liked to have her presence known was all. That and she was quite proud of the new gown she had just flown in from the coast. The blood-red fabric with accents of black lace made her feel bold with their skillfully sewn patterns and matching parasol to hold back the heat from the midday sun. She spun her umbrella to distract the pastor, blew him a kiss, then kicked up a heel as she spun and was on her way back to the saloon.

* * *

Parishioners filed out, one by one thanking Brother Thomas for his words and swooning over his touch as he shook their hands. He loved to hear his own voice. It didn't matter much what he was saying. It was his prideful indulgence. He had few of those. At least that he would let on to his faithful followers. The Word was always much better when he interpreted it in his fashion. The sins could be twisted, the verses moved around, and few of them would notice in the moment since not all could read, and most just waited on his words to guide them anyway.

He waved the last followers out of the doorway and returned to the apse, barren of superfluous decor. This was his quiet moment of his most sacred day. His sermons always took a bite out of him, so having the quiet moments to recharge his social coffers was important.

"Preacher!" Brother Thomas spun on his heels, startled by the abrupt entrance and breaking of his solitude by the panting interloper.

"What is it, my boy? What could be so important that you enter my house with such rash bluster?"

The boy slowed to a halt a few feet in front of Brother Thomas and leaned over, setting his hands upon his knees to hold himself up as he struggled to catch his breath. Brother Thomas approached him, a hint of concern in his tone now. "Breathe, my son, breathe. Your words are no good to me if you can't get them past your lips." The preacher lay a hand on the gasping boy's back. He could feel the rattle of mucus in his lungs, and the dampness of sweat made Brother Thomas recoil a bit and reclaim his hand wiping it on his trousers.

"It's... Remus." The boy's head dropped down again, wheezing and gasping to reclaim his breath.

"Yes, what about him? Has he returned from his wayward pilgrimage?"

The boy shook his head rapidly.

"Well, what kind of trouble has he gotten himself into now?"

The boy breathed in slow and out slow, working to fill his lungs now that the panic of flight was leaving his body. "He's dead."

Brother Thomas's chin quivered in disbelief. "You must be mistaken, boy. You don't just come in my sanctum this way and spew your vile lies. Why I'll have your father--"

"It's not a lie." The boy stood, his hands pressing in on his sides to stave off the impending cramp from his exertion. "Jimmy Joe just got back from his weekly run over the pass. He said he came upon a wrecked coach. You know the one that went missing a while back?" He looked to Brother Thomas for acknowledgment. The preacher gave a gentle nod. "Well, there were bodies all around and one of them was Remus." His voice had regained a normal cadence now. "He was in the middle of the whole mess just lying there naked as the day he were born."

Brother Thomas swayed a bit, stepping away from the boy as each word hit him like a prize fighter's jab. He stumbled as his heels caught on the stair that under the altar and his knees gave out. He sat down with a thud, his world spinning around him. "You must be mistaken. Remus would never... I mean, it's been so long since any of us saw him. How can they be certain that it was him?" He brushed back a wisp of silver-white hair that had tumbled forward over his brow when he landed.

"Oh, it's him, alright. It was hard to recognize his face and all, seeing as his head was all messed up, but he still had the brand on his palm. You know the one you gave—"

"The one he earned for betraying his fellowship?" The shock of the news was gone now, and Brother Thomas was back. He stood and brushed out the crisp white linen suit he wore.

"Y-y-yes. That one. It was there as clear as the day you laid it upon him." The boy was nervous, bowing his head so as not to insult the great figure before him.

"What's this about his head, then?"

"Brother?"

"You said that there was something amiss about his head a moment ago." He smirked his disapproval and turned on his heel to pace around his altar.

"Oh. Well, not to offend, but his head had been split clean open. I'm pretty sure that is at least part of why he is no longer with us."

"What else about the wound?"

"Yeah. There seemed to be a lady's dressing mirror inside the skull. They said it looked as if it had been forced in and it pressed its way out."

"That is odd, don't you think my son?"

"Yessir."

Thomas made another pass around his altar as he contemplated everything the boy had just told him. He closed the massive Bible that lay open at its center and walked back to face the boy. "I would like you to find out as much as you can about that carriage. Can you do that for me, my son?"

"Um, y-yes, sir. I can do that. What exactly do you want to know?"

"I want to know names of the poor souls who met their end on that stage that day and if there happens to be anyone who managed to survive."

"Survive?"

"Yes. I would like to offer my condolences to anyone who might have lost a loved one that day."

"Of course." The boy bowed his head again and began to back himself out of the church.

"And boy."

He stopped and raised his head. "Yes sir?"

"Keep this between us for now. There is no need to upset the congregation with such news of my brother meeting his end this way. I will be sure to say my prayers for the fallen. Our congregants have plenty to worry about in their own lives."

"Will do. Thank you, father."

Brother Thomas waved the boy off so he could make his exit.

The boy backed away slowly and didn't turn until he had reached the threshold of the door. He spun and ran to go inquire about the lost carriage to the coach service.

Brother Thomas turned his back to the door and sobbed. The trials he and his orphan brother had faced growing up. Back then, Thomas was known by another name but still had his eyes on building a kingdom. He and his brother had worked so hard to scrape together their lives after they were abandoned. So young were Remus and Romulus. Taken in by a wolf and fed and kept warm during the cold winter. They were nourished by the wolf's milk and warm coat. The two developed certain traits of their new brethren.

They would run and play and kill with their adopted mother. They grew strong and found that on some nights they would be taken by a change and an insatiable hunger. Over time their monthly changes were contained and they had control of when and whom would see them as their more animalistic selves.

It was when they disagreed about the future of their little hamlet that Romulus cast his brother out into the night, branding him with their family crest and taking up a new moniker for himself. That of Brother Thomas. That is when he began to age and adapt the frailer exterior that his congregants saw now, having suppressed his wolfly nature for so long that it had eaten away at him from the inside.

As the door closed behind the sprinting boy, Thomas's howl of remorse was masked by the walls of his church. Inside, the pews rattled from his roar of anguish at the loss of his brother.

24

Even on a Sunday, there was work to be done. Since the vein of gold was discovered in the nearby hills and the routing of the new train tracks was established, Brainard was alive with fresh faces arriving to make their fortunes each day.

Ruby bounced along through the dusty street, nodding and bidding hello to the shop keepers and horsemen as they went about their business. She acknowledged past, present, and future clients with flirty winks. She liked Dry Bed. It was full of life and the town appreciated her many talents. Her appetites were mostly fed with the random criminal that needed disposing of, or in a pinch, a clandestine visit out to a farm for a lamb or calf should the hunger call.

Hank's was a boisterous saloon on the other end of town. The townsfolk allowed the den of sin to survive because much of the town either frequented it or lived with someone who did. A couple years ago, when the railroad investors showed interest in the little town, it was necessary to upgrade the dingy shack that housed the town drunks into Hank's, which on a good night catered to around a hundred patrons comfortably with music, gambling, whiskey, and beer.

Ruby approached Hank's. She stepped up to the plank walkway, closed her lace parasol, and pushed through the swinging doors. The smell from smoke and alcohol-stained floorboards wafted past her. The door swung closed behind her.

The room was built to house a myriad of tables for patrons to drink or play cards. The bar was on the far wall and took up most of the wall with dark bottles and a large mirror. The intricately carved wooden bar with its smooth marble top was the pride of Hank and a lot prettier than his scarred features.

Hank stood behind the bar diligently swabbing the glass ware. He walked with a limp and the left side of his face was pockmarked with welts and blemishes from his days in the mine. An accident with a stick of dynamite ended his days of going down below. Lucky for him, when he came to, he was coated in and surrounded by a healthy dusting of gold nuggets which he filled his pockets with, blood dripping from his wounds, all while his friends scrambled to dig through the rubble to rescue him.

He left the mines and built the saloon and never looked back.

Ruby, a smile on her lips and a swing in her hips, walked to the bar. Hank's good eye caught her reflection in the mirror next to him.

"Usual?" Hank paused his drying.

"Make it a double. Could use something to wash this taste out of my mouth."

"Thought you didn't take morning clients."

"Your wife is always an exception."

"You'd be doing God's work then, ugly as she is."

"You're one to talk."

Hank grunted. He turned, placed the newly shined glass in front of Ruby. He grabbed a bottle of whiskey from below the counter and poured a generous serving.

Ruby smiled and lifted the glass to her lips. Not a drop

escaped her steady hand as she downed the drink in a single gulp.

"You know, the clean glass makes a big difference," she said.

"Oh yeah?"

"Yep. No backwash to mask the dross you serve. Maybe don't swab so good next time."

"You are an onery cuss, isn't ya."

"The oneriest, handsome."

They chuckled together and Hank refilled her glass with a single shot.

"So, anything new with your friend the preacher?"

"He's still full of shit, but nothing too exciting today."

"I don't know why you insist on hassling him. Eventually he'll turn his sights and his followers towards you, and I can only protect you so much." Hank resumed swabbing empty glasses.

"Your sweet, hon, but I can take care of myself. I've dealt with his kind before and I assure you, if push comes to shove, I'll eat him alive." Ruby gave him a wink and threw down her second shot. "I hear there's a new girl starting up tonight."

"Yeah, you hear right."

"So, what's the poor girl's name?"

"Juliette, I think."

"You think? Was the interview not very memorable?" Ruby smirked.

"Enough of that. You know I don't make the newbies do anything they don't wanna do. Just need to make sure I am advertising appropriately when I chat up the customers is all."

Hank blushed.

"Well, if you're done scaring the poor girl, you know I can always give her the lay of the land."

"That's the word on the street." The two chuckled.

Ruby finished her whiskey and went upstairs to freshen up for her evening in the saloon. *No rest for the wicked.*

Ruby and Juliette

25

Ruby watched from her usual perch on the second floor of the saloon. The evening was much like every other aside from the new girl, Juliette, stalking around the room. Ruby observed as she coyly flirted and sipped on whiskey, on the prowl for her evenings earnings. Ruby was impressed with how easily the woman interacted with the men and women who frequented the saloon.

Juliette was in control of her environment. She was playful but not pushy and very natural with her conversation. She had an air of education about her, but without the piety that often came with it. She liked the new girl, even if she hadn't officially met her yet.

As entertaining as watching the crowd was, Ruby was ready to get to work. She threw back the last of her whiskey and headed to the bar. As easily as Juliette engaged with the customers, Ruby was even smoother. She held court over her domain and the customers made her a path vying for her attention.

She set her empty glass down, signaling Hank for a refill.

"Anyone you got your eye on tonight, Ruby?" Hank asked as he topped off her glass.

"Keeping my options open so far."

"Whiskey?" Juliette had appeared next to Ruby. Hank gave her a nod. "Thanks, hon." She took the glass and downed it.

"Girl after my own heart." Ruby followed suit. She set the glass on the counter and nodded for Hank to fill them both up again.

"You two are gonna drain my reserves before the night is done."

"We're just trying to save the rest of these lambs from having to strip their throats with your moonshine." Juliette said with a wink. "Besides," she slugged her second shot, "You know we're good for it." She winked and signaled another refill.

"I'll leave the bottle. I got actual customers to take care of, you know." Hank gave a halfhearted smirk, left the bottle, and went to tend to the rest of his patrons.

"Well, that was nice of him." Juliette said.

"He just knows better than to try and go back-and-forth too much. He always leaves sad when he stays too long."

The two chuckled. "Wanna grab a table? I'd love to get to know the new face on the block." Ruby said.

"Follow me, hon." Juliette grabbed the bottle and headed toward the empty table in the corner.

The two drank and laughed the night away. Ruby talked mostly about her various experiences with customers, and Juliette talked of her life before the saloon and her current taste for the work that led her to take up residence at the saloon. They entertained each other through the evening instead of powering through the Wednesday evening crowd for a few pennies.

When it was time to retire, empty bottles clinked and rattled against their empty glasses. Their ability to put away that much of Hank's hooch and remain upright would fuel many a teetotaler's gossip mill for weeks to come.

"Well, I'm over here." Juliette motioned to her room a couple doors down from Ruby.

"And I'm right here. Good to finally meet the new girl."

"Pleasure was all mine." Juliette grinned and turned toward her room. She hesitated, turned back to Ruby. "You know, if you ever get bored and want a friend, my door's always open."

Ruby gave her a sweet smile. "If my sheets are ever cold, I'll be sure to come a-knocking." She gave her a sly wink and blew her a kiss. Then she turned and went into her room.

Juliette gave a girlish giggle, then spun back towards her room and left the noise of the saloon behind her as the door shut.

She unsnapped her black lace corset. The relief of the pressure being released made her sigh.

"You really should consider locking your door, my dear. You never know what type of folks are wandering around a house of sin such as this."

Juliette startled at the unannounced visitor. He was tall with white and gray hair. He sat in the corner by her lamp, its pale yellow light highlighting his crisp white linen suit. She could smell his age from her side of the room.

"Jesus! What are you doing in here?" She said, not letting him break her stride for longer than a second as she continued to relieve the stressed buttons on her corset.

"Jesus is why I'm here, my child." Brother Thomas stood. His wiry figure towered above her. His wispy white hair clung to his scalp, held down by the perspiration that beaded atop his liver-spotted head.

"It's been a long night and I'm tired, preacher, so why don't we have whatever this conversation is another time? I'm not in the mood to play hide the sacrament with you."

"Very colorful language. But I hope you know I'm here to help you to follow a truer path."

"Pretty sure I'm on a path that's plenty true. No deception happening between these thighs. Just good old-fashioned sinning." She unclasped the last of the snaps and laid her corset across the foot of her bed. She made her way to her vanity and sat. She worked the hair pins from her long black hair. It fell across her shoulders. Thomas came up behind her.

"Everybody sins, my dear. But how do you go about atoning? That's the question." A leer twitched at the corner of his thin lips. He placed a pale, clammy hand on her shoulder.

"Oh, don't you worry about me, preacher, and I'm pretty sure I didn't ask for you to lay hands on me this evening." Juliette was no longer amused by the hypocritical visit from Thomas.

She had heard from a couple other girls about these drop-ins by the local man of God. It was his way of keeping tabs on the local flesh peddlers and to exert power in his own way. "Maybe you should worry more about your flock then about getting your hands on mine." She took a hair pin, gently slid it under his hand on her shoulder and pushed his hand off.

"I think you don't understand what I am offering you, child." He moved away and over to her bed. He scooped up her corset and traced the intricate lace pattern between his fingers.

"First off, I'm not your child," she turned to faced him and stood up. "Second, you haven't paid for the honor of running your greasy fingers across my wares, so why don't you be a good boy and scuttle back to your cave." Juliette snatched the corset from his fingers and flung it over her shoulder.

"Now you're being rude." His eyes hardened. In a quick motion he flung the back of his hand across her cheek. Taken by surprise, Juliette dropped to the floor, dazed from the sting from his bony hand. "We could have been friends had you allowed me to bear witness for you." He reached down and grabbed a mass of hair on the back of her head, lifting her up. She stood defiant before him, her jaw set, fists balled by her sides, and resolution in her stance showing she would not be caught by surprise again. "Now I'll just have to lay my sacrament upon you." He wound back to slap her again and swung. His strike was cut short, close enough to her cheek he could feel the delicate peach fuzz of her skin on his palm.

"You don't want to do this, preacher." A low growl rumbled beneath the surface of her threat.

"You best let go before I lose my patience with you." His voice quavered as he fought the unexpected strength of her grip.

She stared into his eyes. A smirk crept up one side of her face, then the other, widening and baring her teeth. Her canines pressed forward a bit as her inner wolf stirred.

He was shaking now as he tried to free his hand from her grip. "That's quite enough."

"I think it's time we put a finger on what the real problem is here, preacher." Juliette secured his arm with both hands. She squeezed his arm. He let go of her hair and grasped his captured arm. The pain grew and his knees weakened. He sank to the ground. "Please stop!" He could hold back a scream no longer.

Juliette opened her mouth and guided his second and third fingers into her mouth. She looked into his eyes as she closed her mouth around his fingers. Her teeth gnashed through his paper-like skin and the crunch of bone rattled in her head, drowning out his calls for help. She severed the fingers with little effort. She fought the urge to strip the fingers of their flesh and enjoy the quick snack. She let loose her grip and he pulled away. Blood spurted from his freed hand. In a single bite, she had stripped him of his pride and his power. She pulled back, blood streaming down her chin. The man looked up from his bleeding, misshapen hand into her smiling, canine-like eyes. She spit his inert fingers into his face. "Your body and blood, offered up to forgive your sins."

Thomas shrieked, clutching his hand to stem the bleeding. Blood spurted through his fingers, staining his pristine white suit. He stood and attempted to make it out her door, but the shock was setting in, and he stumbled, falling to his face. His panic mounted as he struggled to right himself. He yelped as pain shot though his body from the fresh wound. He stumbled and slipped around in his own blood.

Juliette wiped her forearm across her chin and tongue to scrape the sour taste of him away. "Get your hypocritical ass out of my room, you grotesque fuck." She stepped over the whimpering man and opened her door, not caring that she grazed his wounded hand as she did. His yelps made her grin mischievously.

She went to the railing of the walkway. "Hank!" The small late-night crowd hushed as they took sight of the bloody woman.

"Juliette? You okay?"

"Yeah, but I think your preacher's misunderstood the definition of fingering."

Her words were echoed by the high-pitched yelps of the emasculated man squirming on her floor.

"Jonus!" Hank hollered for the bar boy.

"Yessir?" A tall man of about nineteen looked up from the poker game he was overseeing. Hank pointed up at Juliette. "Oh, shit!"

"Git up there and see what happened." Hank barked.

Jonus wove through the maze of empty tables on his way to the stairs.

Ruby stood two doors down from Juliette, hair mussed and adorned in a silk robe. She looked past the girl to the bleeding mess on her floor. She grinned. The two women locked eyes and Ruby gave Juliette a quiet nod. Juliette answered back with a nod of her own.

"Oh God!" Jonus broke their eye contact as he got up the stairs and looked past her into Juliette's room. "Jesus! What happened?"

"He came up for a bite but didn't like the menu." She dabbed at the corners of her mouth.

"Hank! I'm gonna need some help. And someone go wake the doc." Jonus pushed past Juliette to tend to the injured man.

"Also, Hank?" Juliette got the owner's attention. "I'm gonna need a new room. This one's been sullied."

She walked back to her room to gather her things, stepping over the sobbing man in his blood-spattered white suit.

26

The doctor was able to provide little comfort for the preacher beyond the couple of laudanum vials he had on hand. He did his best to sew up the ravaged area but salvaging the fingers was beyond the doctor's grasp.

The local lawman was brought in, on request of Thomas' congregants, but he was well aware of Thomas' penchant for providing confession to the new girls at the saloon.

"Miss, I'm gonna ask ya to keep yer teeth to yourself from now on."

"But that's what they pay the most for." Juliette fired back.

The Sherriff stifled a laugh. "Just try to keep outta trouble, can ya?"

"Will do." She gave him a coquettish smile and impishly crossed her heart.

Hank let Juliette have the room next to Ruby. The two now shared a balcony and Juliette's handling of the preacher had elicited Ruby's full respect. When the two were not entertaining clients, they built their friendship through long evening conversations over whiskey on their balcony. The two were nearly inseparable, opting to shop, dine, and sometimes even entertain together.

Their zeal for the business was similar, and their carnal

tastes provided higher fees and a reputation that grew beyond the borders of their little railroad stop of a town.

Ruby was puzzled by Juliette's monthly disappearances. She figured it was tied to her womanly cycle but didn't know why she would completely disappear for three to four days without word. Juliette always changed the subject when Ruby brought it up.

The troubles with the preacher quieted. After a few weeks the greasy old man returned to his duties and appeared none the worse for wear, aside from the bulbous wrapping that encased his hand where missing digits should be. He had asked his congregants to not only avoid the saloon interactions with Juliette, but to pretend the whole awful incident had never occurred.

They were good sheep and returned with zeal to his pews.

The other odd occurrence in town was a recent uptick in animal attacks on the livestock. There had always been trouble with coyotes and wolves, but of late, there appeared to be an uptick in disappearances and kills. The cattle and sheep, if they were found, had massive wounds too brutal for a singular wolf, but there was little evidence of anything else. What was even more odd was the lack of animal signs around the kill sites. There was always a lot of mussed earth around the kill but rarely animal tracks. Some farmers started to suspect a bear.

The irony of Juliette's bite was that it did little more than wake the dormant beast in Thomas. His cravings were awakened but with a new focus; to bring about the world Remus was ostracized for envisioning. A world of wolves where humans were cattle and the strong would rule over all. The humiliation he faced at the saloon amplified his need to humiliate and tame Juliette and the other bar girls, but he would bide his time and build his pack before approaching her again.

27

"Children, I say to you, the den of evil and sin that is down the street must be cleansed. Some of my flock is known to partake in the carnal offerings beyond the threshold of this sanctuary. I am not here to judge ye. That is for the Lord to weigh your soul upon your reckoning. But to those that taint our good town with their evil, it is our will to ensure their deeds do not seep from their keep like an untended infection, festering and rotting the collective soul of our town. They must be sanitized so as not to infect us further with their putrid ways."

The doting followers nodded and swayed, mumbling their amens in response. The church was their realm but since the Thomas incident at the saloon he had been asking his followers to join him in evening rituals out in his barn. It was always an honor to be selected as only one or two of his flock were brought in for each session.

"I'm sure you have all noticed my inner circle has grown." With a flourish from his clumsily bandaged hand, he recognized a group of four men who sat servile and rigid behind him. "These chosen few are to be at my right hand when the Rapture ensues. Yes, my children, a reckoning is coming, and we have the choice to vanquish or be vanquished." The pews resonated with a monotone *Amen.*

"Brothers and sisters. As we build towards the cleansing, know that soon we will be strong enough to take this town back and rid it of the grotesque filth that infects our very souls. After we purge this town of the unclean, we will rise up and cleanse the earth like the ripples from a pebble dropped in a pond." The followers behind the preacher sat with wide grins and blank eyes. They had been taken in by the preacher after the incident and been shown his inner light. They were made part of his army and given insight into his grand plan. They would be gods among men and the four horsemen of his own apocalypse.

"So, what can you do to prepare yourselves for the reckoning?" He raised his eyebrow, a bead of sweat clung to the ridge of his brow for a moment before diving to the ground. "You can stay diligent. You can keep your alms flowing so that the church may be able to build and rebuild after the reckoning. You can stay true to your voice from God and follow me to the abyss as I fight for this town and the good people in it." He accented his words with the pounding of his bandaged fist on the lectern as if hammering a gavel.

The hum of *Amens* grew and rolled through the crowd. The chapel was alive with the power of the preacher's words.

"Now, let us sing our praise to the Lord which we exalt and look inward when asked to do his bidding so that we may know that the acts that we do are in his name and that no evil can ever be done in the name of our God. Sister Margaret, will you please lead us in song?"

Margaret blushed at being recognized by Thomas and gave a shy nod as she stood, turned, and faced the congregants. "Shall we all sing, 'Farewell to Sin?'"

"Fine choice, my sister." He gestured to begin. A syrupy grin spread across his sweaty face.

I will part with thee, old master;
This is my firm resolve;
And I'll boldly state my reason,
Why we must now dissolve.

The wages of sin is death,
The wages of sin is death,
The wages of sin is death, and woe,
And bitter remorse; I've found it so;
Bitter, bitter,
Bitter remorse and woe.

I have served thee long and faithful,
Confessed you were my lord;
All your way was dark and painful,
And what is my reward?

The wages of sin is death,
The wages of sin is death,
The wages of sin is death, and woe,
And bitter remorse; I've found it so;
Bitter, bitter,
Bitter remorse and woe.

I have given time and talents,
My health and honor, too,
And exposed my soul to torments,
And what did you bestow?

The wages of sin is death,
The wages of sin is death,
The wages of sin is death, and woe,
And bitter remorse; I've found it so;
Bitter, bitter,
Bitter remorse and woe.

You have flattered me, and promised
Much pleasure in your reign;
I have sowed and reaped your harvest,
Now what my wretched gain?

The wages of sin is death,
The wages of sin is death,
The wages of sin is death, and woe,
And bitter remorse; I've found it so;
Bitter, bitter,
Bitter remorse and woe.

The room rang with verse after verse. The longer it went the louder the congregants sang. Brother Thomas swelled with each syllable. As the timbre rose, he hummed, his smile stretching wider with every refrain. He craned his neck and aimed his voice skyward and emanated a clear toned "Aaaaaahhhhhoooooooohhhhhh." His howls soared over the crowd and fueled their zeal. He was soon joined by his four horsemen, raising their song to a roar at the word of death.

28

Susan dropped her sticky ball of dough into the cauldron. A poof of flour colored the air above the pot's rim. Her fire cracked and popped in eager anticipation of the rustic loaf.

Henry rocked his chair. The dim glow of tobacco embers gently hissed at the mouth of his pipe. His book was illuminated by the candle that flickered next to him on a small table.

Their cozy house was warm from the fire, and clean from the meticulous care Susan took to make sure their humble space was comfortable. She hated the grit under her bare toes from dirt and gravel stowing away on Henry's boots after a long day tending their land. She ensured the worn planks they walked on were free of the soil beyond their door.

The metallic clank of Susan fitting the lid on the pot rang through the sparse room. She lifted the heavy pot and set it on the worn hook of the swing arm and used her wrought iron poker to maneuver the bread into place over the fire. Soon the inviting smell of flour and yeast would tickle their nostrils. Susan always enjoyed the process of kneading and baking bread, and a loaf would last the two of them for days.

Their home was clean and humble, the main room taken up mostly by the hand-crafted table Henry had built as a wedding gift for Susan. Many meals were prepared and eaten there, and Susan took pride in the fine wood grain of the smooth planks. It was a symbol of not only the union she shared with Henry, but of the long life she planned to share with the man that tended their fields and that one day would cradle their children.

Susan turned from the fire and met her husband's eyes. The corner of her mouth winked at him with a warm smile, and he returned the gesture with a gentle puff on his pipe and a playful kiss blown through the air with a soft cloud of pipe smoke.

BANG-BANG-BANG!

They started at the jarring rattle of unsolicited rapping on their door. It was out of the ordinary for them to receive guests, let alone unannounced visitors, so close to dinner time. They resided on the outskirts of Dry Bed, a good thirty-minute gallop from town on a fresh horse, making visitors a rarity.

They looked to each other, confused and unsettled. A wisp of hair had sprung loose from Susan's tight bun and she pressed it away from her face as she worked it smooth again with the rest of the auburn locks that were pulled back in the tight formation.

"Who could that be?" She asked Henry.

"Not sure. Were you expecting someone this evening?" He pulled his pipe from between his teeth. The warmth from the hot tobacco heated his hand as he looked to the door to see if the knocking was perhaps from the wind. But there had been little more than a breeze, let alone a gust worthy of disturbing their heavy door in such a way.

BANG-BANG-BANG!

Another heavy knock. Henry stood. He set his book down with his pipe laid between the worn pages to keep his place. The candle flickered frantically. He stepped toward the door.

Susan stood by the fire, her hand on the table so lovingly crafted by Henry, taking comfort in the smooth texture of the varnished planks.

Henry approached the door, and a third knocking shook the heavy wood. "Who's there?" Henry's voice boomed. He was not a violent man and there was no anger in his cadence. But his height and natural barrel chest made for a resonant, intimidating baritone timber that resonated through the small room.

No one answered. But another rap, this time more urgent, rattled the hinges.

"Henry?" Susan's voice trembled.

Henry turned to her and shifted his protective tone to sooth her nerves, "It's okay, my love." He turned back to the door. "Who's there?" He barked, his tone more urgent this time. Dry Bed was known to play host to some rough and tumble types, especially these days with the nearing railway. The sheriff, however, kept a tight grip on troublemakers. An encounter of this nature, especially this far outside the city's boundaries, was unexpected.

Henry kept his Winchester hunting rifle nestled against the door jamb. He didn't like the idea of turning its deadly barrel on another man but was not about to be threatened in his own home. He plucked up the weapon and chambered a round. Susan jumped at the sharp click. He hoped the metallic sound of his rifle being primed would be enough warning that whoever was causing trouble would think twice and turn tail before the situation escalated.

"I'm not gonna ask again. If you're not a friend, then you best be on your way!"

The room was quiet except for nervous breaths from Susan and the heavy pounding of Henry's heart thumping in his ears.

BANG-BANG-BANG!

Henry laid his hand on the latch, his gun balanced in his other hand. He pulled the door open and swung his rifle up to with his eyeline. But he was aiming at air. The dark purple of evening was heavy on the horizon. The stars twinkled beyond the awning that sheltered the door from the elements. The sharp chirp of crickets was all Henry heard.

"What is it, Henry?" Susan asked.

He didn't answer. His eyes darted right and left. He looked all around and took a step forward. He was half in and half out. There was nothing there. He kept his rifle at the ready as he listened for shuffling footsteps or anything that would give away the trickster who was harassing them. He waited for a few more moments, quietly staring into the dark and holding his breath. He exhaled slowly, relaxed his finger from the trigger, and lowered his weapon. He turned to Susan; a nervous grin twitched across his face.

"It's just the wind, I guess." He chuckled.

Susan sighed and nervously giggled. They both laughed, filling the room with their released tension. Henry let his guard down. He took a step back into the house, his Winchester hanging from his hand. Susan turned back to the fire and to the bread that was baking in the black cauldron.

Suddenly, Henry's laughter was gone. Susan didn't notice at first as she was still shaking off her nerves with her own chuckles. But his laughter had been replaced with a splash. Susan turned to see Henry's headless torso twitching in the doorway. Blood sprayed into the air, coating the door frame in Henry. The tendons in his hand tightened and the rifle roared, splintering the pristine floorboards next to his dying body. Susan's brain struggled to process the vision of her beloved *sans* head as his body fell first to its knees and then thumped down on the floor, a misty fountain of blood arcing through the room, the last of his life varnishing the floorboards in sticky crimson.

She screamed and backed against the fireplace. Her left hand, reaching for support, grasped the hot swing arm. Her flesh sizzled at the touch of the wrought iron, and she screamed in pain. She looked at the beet-red line branded on her palm and whimpered. She grabbed a towel from the table and quickly wrapped it around her throbbing hand.

Her screams were accompanied by the scrape of claws on the floorboards. The dim light of their cabin glistened on the bloodied claws and fur that enveloped the creature silhouetted in the doorway. The gray-streaked fur stank of musk. The creature towered over Henry's body. Susan searched for an opening to run past the beast but as it stood to its height, its muscled body claimed the entire opening and reached almost to the ceiling.

Susan kept her eyes on the creature while she searched for the poker with her hands. She ignored the pain from the burn as she grasped and raised the pointed implement towards the beast. She swung it in front of her with panicked futility. She was a fighter. She had fought her whole life, and no demon was going to take her without a fight.

A low rumble rattled in the creature's throat as it drew its lips back from its yellowed teeth. The evil smile stretched wide. Saliva dripped down onto Henry's back. Its teeth parted revealing a massive dark maw. One hand was misshapen with two of its middle digits only partly formed. It raised the other clawed hand and Susan noticed something dangled from the tips of its talons. It was Henry's disembodied head. Her husband's twitching hazel eyes stared back at her. The creature brought the head to its face and lapped at the dripping neck hole, coating its tongue and mouth in inky red.

Susan cried, then reached deep inside. She stood, raised the poker to swing. Her cries shifted to anger as she charged the massive beast. It grinned and appeared to chuckle at the bleak effort of its prey. Henry's head dropped to the floor as Susan swung for home.

The night air filled with Susan's yelps and screams as the animal pulled her apart. The tearing of fabric and flesh filled the room as the pridefully clean abode was painted in the lovers blood from top to bottom.

29

"Hank, I'm gonna be gone for a few days. Need out of the hubbub for a bit." Juliette had come down from her room and was sitting at the bar.

"Damnit, Juliette. On a weekend? You know I need all of you ladies to be here when the railroad workers are off?"

"Oh, come on. It's not like someone else can't handle 'em."

"I know they can handle them, but one less body in a bed means that after a while those assholes start to look to *me* for entertainment."

"We both know that's not true." She gestured to Hank's face.

"That's not right and you know it."

"You know I find scars sexy. Don't worry about the weekend. It'll be fine."

"Leaving us again? That mean I get your high rollers for the weekend?" Ruby asked.

"Sure. They always come back to me anyway. I think you scare them a bit."

"I do, in fact. But only when they ask real nice."

"Ruby, can you talk some sense into her?" Hank pleaded. He plucked three shot glasses from under the bar. He lined them up and poured a round.

Ruby took up the healthy pour and toasted. "Not my circus, not my monkeys." She tossed back the whiskey and motioned Juliette to follow her upstairs.

Juliette downed her drink and fell in behind Ruby. "I'll be back in a few days, and we can talk about it then Hank."

Hank shook his head, collected the dirty glasses and wiped down the rest of the bar.

"You really gotta go this weekend?" Ruby asked. She had taken a liking to Juliette, which was unusual for her. Since the Braided Pony, Ruby had wanted little to do with relationships. Even though she really didn't have anyone this close there. They headed up the stairs.

"It's for the best, I promise. Besides its only for a few days." She placed her palm gently on Ruby's back.

"Maybe I could go with you then?"

"I would love nothing more, but I need this time alone or I turn into a real beast."

"I get that. I've been known to tear someone a new one before."

They reached the top of the stairs and Juliette grabbed Ruby's hand and turned her face to face. "Once I get back, maybe we can spend a little more time together. Just the two of us, what do you think?"

"I think you're playing dangerously with the moral compass of the fine folks in this town asking me that question." Ruby, even while warning Juliette, grasped her hand firmly and pulled her closer.

"What happens behind closed doors, no one has to know about." Juliette looked into Ruby's eyes and coyly bit her lip.

"Fine, you little brat. Leave me alone to face this place all alone. But don't think I'm giving back any of your regulars so easy."

Ruby kissed the air between them playfully and went into her room.

30

Ruby watched Juliette from the balcony outside her room as she made her way down the street to the livery.

"Fuck it. Where are you going?" Ruby stood up and headed down the stairs in pursuit of Juliette.

She stayed out of sight the entire trek. Juliette had taken a path out of Dry Bed that Ruby was already familiar with. It happened to be the route that Ruby took to get into town when she left Thrall. It was not so much a defined trail, as a natural path down the mountains and through the valley that opened up to the little town. Ruby took note of the familiar spaces and continued to track Juliette by her scent.

Along with the scent of Juliette, Ruby caught the scent of another animal aside from Juliette's mount. She had taken along a cow. Ruby guessed that Juliette might have a hermit relative outside town that she'd visit with gifts each month. That would explain the cow for sure.

Ruby noticed another curiosity. Juliette had an aroma that Ruby always found pleasant and inviting. A distinctly human scent that Ruby had learned to identify over her centuries of hunting. This morning though, something was different. It was familiar in that it was still Juliette, but there was something else there. A pungent underlying scent mixed with her natural pheromones. It was not off putting to Ruby, just different. It was not something a human would be able to detect, but Ruby certainly had identified the change.

She followed the scent into the thick trees along the river. They traveled most of the day and the heat was edging up in the final days of Spring. It was already late in the afternoon, verging on evening, when Ruby noticed Juliette's scent growing stronger. She believed she was getting close to Juliette. She marveled at the connection to her past trip, as she had been taken almost all the way back to the cabin where she had killed the young couple. In fact, it was the same cabin coming into view through the thick trees.

Ruby dismounted and tied off her mount. The horse chuffed as the wind changed and it picked up on the scent Ruby had noticed. She patted its neck to calm it.

The forest stirred all around the cabin. Ruby was used to wildlife not being a fan of hers, but it was obvious that forest's uncharacteristic quiet had started before she got there. The quiet fed her curiosity along with the growth of the new scent.

The shadows grew long as the sun traveled beyond the horizon. In these early days of summer, the night came later, but also more intensely.

Ruby approached the rundown cabin and smiled at the thought of the meals she had lucked upon the last time she was there. It didn't look like anyone had taken up residence since. There were signs of some campers or hunters that used the shelter from time to time, but no established squatters as far as Ruby could discern.

A thin trail of white smoke leaked out of the stone chimney but there was no smell of dinner being prepped. Just outside the door, the cow that Juliette had brought along was secured to a tree. It munched idly on the surrounding grass and wildflowers.

Ruby made her way to the door, her curiosity fully piqued. Daylight dimmed and the moon would soon be up to light the cloudless night.

Ruby had no fear of what she might encounter. Being back to her full strength, if there was some ill that would befall her and/or Juliette in the middle of the forest, she was more than prepared to deal with it. She approached the door and knocked. Any shuffling sounds she made out coming from inside halted. Juliette did not answer immediately. Ruby knocked again.

"Go away! Travelers aren't welcome here." Juliette barked at the interloper.

"That's a bit terse, don't you think?"

"Jesus. Ruby? Is that you?"

"Who else would follow you out into the middle of nowhere? Now open the door."

"Oh God! Ruby, you've gotta go. Get on your horse and ride out of here now!"

"I'm not leaving until we talk."

"Ruby, get the fuck out of here!"

"Had I known you had such a mouth I woulda had way more respect for you, my love."

The door flung open, startling Ruby. She took a step back. "I said leave!" Juliette's voice was thick, her eyes were wild and blood shot, and she stood before Ruby, her nude body silhouetted by the dusk and the glow of the fire inside.

"What the hell are you doing out here?"

"I can't bear the possibility of something happening to you. Please leave!" She took a step forward and gave Ruby a shove to get her moving.

Ruby tumbled backward both because she was not ready for the assault, but also, Juliette was stronger than Ruby had expected. They had spent a lot of time together over the months both in and out of the bedroom and Juliette never presented such power.

Ruby sat on the ground. Her friend stood above her panting and agitated. "I'm not here to hurt you, Juliette. I just want to know what's going on?"

Juliette answered with a roar that was part anger, part pain.

"Well, that's new." Ruby said. She rose and dusted herself off.

Juliette clomped towards her waving her arms and grunting, spitting, and acting as if she were possessed.

"Fuck this." Ruby stood firm. She flicked her wrist, and a single talon elongated from her index finger. "Time to relax." She timed a strike with Juliette's chaotic swings and jabbed her claw into Juliette's shoulder injecting her paralytic toxin.

Juliette stopped her flailing and looked down at the talon inserted a good two inches inside her shoulder. A guttural growl rumbled from her gut into her throat. She looked into Ruby's eyes. Juliette used her free hand to grab hold of the claw and slowly pull it from her arm. Ruby was fascinated. Juliette was very strong and the fact that her paralytic didn't work was something she hadn't experienced before.

Juliette clasped Ruby's hand holding up the red tinged talon. She extended her tongue and licked the thin stream of blood that tinted Ruby's claw. Juliette stared into Ruby's eyes with a smirk. She let go and kicked Ruby, chasing after her as she tumbled along, like a twisted game of fetch.

Ruby skidded to a stop on all fours. Dirt and plant remnants riddled her clothes and smeared her face. An angry smile stretched across her elongating mouth. "So, you like it rough. I can do rough." Her long tongue lashed out, lapping at the detritus coloring her forehead. Juliette was still coming for her, her naked curves glistening in the growing moonlight. She looked different somehow, though. Much of her nakedness was being enveloped in a thick layer of fur.

She appeared to be taller, almost six feet now when she normally stood at a little more than five foot. Her fingers sprouted long claws and there was a thin protuberance following her. No, not following her, it was her. She had grown a tail. By the time she was close enough to get the full picture, all Ruby saw was fangs, claws, and fur lashing out at her like a wild animal.

Juliette flew towards Ruby. Ruby rolled to the side to avoid the pounce. She stood ready and watched Juliette tumble into the brush. Juliette yipped her displeasure and scrambled to right herself as she plowed through the undergrowth.

"I know you like it doggy style, but isn't this a bit excessive, Jules?"

Juliette snarled and snapped, spittle frothing from her snout as her frustration built.

"I don't want to hurt you, Jules, but I will if I have to." Juliette pawed the ground, readying another attack. "Jules. Are you in there?"

Juliette's hackles rose, making her appear larger, as the fur on her shoulders bristled. The wolf lunged forward, charging Ruby. Ruby blinked her eyes. They flashed from emerald to pure black. She never liked transforming while wearing clothes. Her inner self had a way of tearing through whatever she was wearing. She held back a bit. She didn't need her full strength just yet. She was not sure how strong Juliette was when she was wolfed out, so she allowed herself to tap into just the outer elements of her powers to see if she could hold her off or find a way to subdue Juliette.

Ruby's fingers stretched, their honed talons sprouted long enough to counter the claws Juliette had grown. Ruby braced for Juliette's impact. The frothing beast hit her, and they went flying. Juliette's mass seemed to have grown ten times since she transformed. The slight, lithe yet buxom friend Ruby was accustomed to, was now sporting about three hundred pounds of fresh muscle and powerful paws with six-inch claws on each of her legs. If she got the upper hand, it would be no problem for her to rabbit kick the hell out of Ruby while chomping away at any available flesh.

Ruby clung to the animal, keeping herself as close to Juliette as she could. She scurried around the large, muscled body, digging her claws in for traction and pulling herself around behind Juliette. "Reminds me of those cowhands from Albuquerque." She strained to hold onto the bucking beast. "You remember them?"

Juliette didn't appear amused. She snapped at the air, hunting for purchase on any bit of Ruby's flesh she could find.

Ruby bore her talons into Juliette's thick trapezius muscles, hoping her friend would heal just as quickly as she had. It was worse, though. Juliette was healing so quickly that Ruby was caught in the growing muscle and sinew. Ruby retracted her claws, tearing gashes in Juliette's back. Ruby kicked off and flew backwards while Juliette continued forward.

Juliette howled as Ruby's claws came loose and her friend launched off her. She continued forward and skidded to a halt about twenty yards on. She shook her head, a mist of blood from her back rose into the air. The moon was bright, making the woods alive with macabre shadows and dark silhouettes. Juliette raised her head and howled her frustration to the skies.

"Well, your singing voice is still about as lovely as before. What say we call it a tie and go have a drink."

Juliette chuffed and snorted. Her back muscles had already healed, and she was ready for another pass. She paced around Ruby, snorting her discontent and chomping at the space between them in frustration.

"You are a miraculous beast. But now it's my turn, my dear." Ruby crossed her arms across her chest and bowed her head. She delved into her inner self and called on the strength she stored up for her kills. She didn't want to hurt Juliette but also didn't want to be her chew toy for the rest of the night. Ruby's hair rose as if charged with electricity. She flung her arms wide, flicking her talons out to their full length. The pop of bone and cartilage expanding and shifting filled the air as Ruby's legs elongated, adding a couple of feet to her height. Her thigh muscles expanded along with her shoulders, feet and chest cavity. She flexed outward and her clothes fell to her feet in shreds. She looked up, her eyes two black mirrors, and her mouth ripped up the sides of her cheeks exposing a maw filled with crooked teeth from front to back, top to bottom. "Okay, baby. Let's play!" She opened her mouth wide and hissed, her elongated tongue whipping the air as an invitation.

Juliette roared. The trees shook and the ground trembled. She bore down and charged. Ruby stood her ground waiting for the beast's impetuous nature to take control. Juliette kicked up a cloud of forest floor as she sped towards Ruby and closed the distance. The distance between them quickly disappeared. Ruby readied herself and lowered her body to the ground. Juliette trampled over her snapping at Ruby as she passed. Ruby felt the warm spray of saliva as Juliette's jaws clamped shut less than an inch from her cheek. Ruby kicked upward, catching Juliette in the belly. She launched Juliette into the air. The wolf somersaulted through the forest and slammed back first into the heavy trunk of a thick pine. The shaken conifer poured down a shower of pine needles. Juliette slid down the trunk and slumped to the ground dazed, her back itching with slivers.

"Who says I don't give good wood."

Juliette stumbled to her feet. She swayed back and forth on all fours, working to regain her balance and to shake off the collision.

"I'm pretty sure we could both do this all night so maybe let's talk-" Juliette had regained her composure more quickly than Ruby expected and used the tree to launch herself at her. She landed center mass and pinned Ruby to a tree.

"Fine, you can be on top." Ruby struggled to get the words out, the air pushed from her lungs by the impact of the massive beast.

Juliette held her there panting, her arms wrapped around the tree in a massive bear hug with Ruby between. Ruby could barely breathe let alone move. Tears gathered in the corners of her eyes as the pressure built in her head. "All right, baby. As much as I like being this close to you, we can't stay like this all night." Ruby wrenched her left hand free. She drove her index talon into Juliette's biceps. Juliette howled and loosened her grip. Ruby's tongue whipped out and wrapped around Juliette's neck. She reeled her in and clamped her mouth around her throat. She constricted her jaw enough to close on Juliette's windpipe but not enough to break it. She kicked her feet down into the Juliette's knee joints, forcing her to the ground. Juliette fought but she couldn't breathe, and Ruby wouldn't let go. Ruby held her in place, the blood flow cut off to her brain and the oxygen grew scant. The beast heaved trying to find her wind again but couldn't. Ruby held her there until her pulse was weak. She let go and the wolf slumped to the ground. Ruby stood over her friend panting. Juliette attempted to rise again but Ruby landed a single blow to the side of her head, knocking her out cold.

"Jesus, Honey. If I'd have known you were this much fun, we would've played much sooner." Ruby dropped to her knees regaining her breath. Her naked body glistened in the bright moonlight. She laid a hand on her friend's fur covered throat and soothed the sleeping beast. She marveled at the quickness of Juliette's healing as the small puncture wounds she had inflicted on her neck filled back in as she caressed. "Sweet dreams, baby. We have a lot to talk about."

31

"Oh, my head." Juliette lay on a cot, eyes squinched, and palm pressed to her forehead.

The cabin was sparse aside from the dust-covered furniture remnants. The body of the man from the cabin had been cleared away, presumably by Juliette when she found the place. Ruby stood by the fireplace readying a pot of coffee.

"Yeah, hangovers are a bitch. You want some coffee?"

"Ruby? What are you doing here? You can't be here. I..." She tried to get up, but her head swam, and she felt she might throw up.

"Yeah, you said all that last night. That's quite the show you put on." Ruby plucked the steeping pot from the fire and poured two cups of coffee. She put the pot next to the fire to stay warm and brought the cups over.

"What did you see?" Juliette groaned, holding her head in one hand and accepting the cup of coffee in the other.

"I saw more of you then I ever have before, and we've entertained together."

"That's impossible. How are you still alive?"

"We all have our secrets." She took a sip of coffee. "Mine's just a little more refined, let's say."

Juliette rolled to her side, setting the coffee on the edge of the cot to steady it. She propped herself up on an elbow and squinted past her pain. "Did I hurt you?"

"Aww. That's sweet. Yes, but I don't hold a grudge. Actually, I do hold grudges, but I'm willing to try not to with you." Ruby winked and took a sip of coffee. "So how long has this been a part of you?"

"My affliction came about a little before I arrived in town."

"So, you're still new to this whole 'I'm a monster' world. Fun, ain't it."

"Don't think I'd call it fun."

"At least you're sexy when you beast out. Holy shit, girl. That was quite a ride."

"We didn't fuck, did we?"

"Not yet, but I'm game if you are. Maybe try to bite a bit less, though." She thought for a moment, "Or not."

"What are you gonna do about my condition?"

"Why do *I* have to do anything? Seems you've got a pretty good system going. I take it Bessie is in case you need a snack?" On cue, a nervous moo came from outside the cabin.

"Yeah. I come up here so I won't hurt anyone."

"I get that. You should really consider livening up the place, though. Maybe a throw rug over there or something." Juliette chuckled. "So, how'd you get to be this way?" Ruby blew a bit of steam off the brim of her cup.

Juliette looked down, embarrassment flashing across her face in the firelight.

"Come on. I'll tell you mine if you tell me yours," Ruby prodded.

"I was on a stagecoach heading to the coast to be with family after my husband died."

"You were married?"

"I was. He was a good man. Not rich, but he took good care of me, and he worked hard. Too hard, I guess. One day he was out plowing. The next thing I knew, he was face down in the dirt. Gone before he even hit the ground.

"After the funeral I had nothing holding me to the land, so I sold everything I could and bought passage cross country. I wanted to start over and escape all the pain that I felt every time I woke up in that house, on that land, and without him."

"So how did this all happen?"

"There was an accident on the stage. Overnight, we were attacked by something. Kind of a wolf but bigger and meaner."

"We've met."

Juliette smirked, took a sip of her cooling coffee and continued. "Well, it was down to me and that thing and somehow I managed to get a hold of my vanity kit and got the son-of-a-bitch to shove the mirror into its own brain."

"Neat trick."

"Yeah, I lost my hand in the process."

"Coulda fooled me."

"Turns out, when it died, it turned into a man, and I ended up with the wolf in me."

"Typical man. Knocks you up and leaves you with the brat."

"Anyway, my hand grew back the next time the moon was full, and I've been dealing with this ever since."

"So, you only change during a full moon?"

"I have a little bit of control over it the rest of the month, but I am strongest and mostly beast during the full moon."

"Hence the disappearing act every month."

"You got it."

They sat and drank their coffee while Ruby digested Juliette's story. "You realize we have a real problem then, right?" Ruby said over her shoulder heading back to refill her coffee.

"What's that?"

"Preacher man is one of you."

"Can't be. Oh shit. I bit him. Oh Jesus. He's insane. If I can do this when I'm a wolf, what is he like, then?"

"If I had to guess, he's a real bitch."

Juliette drained her coffee and looked at Ruby. "I need something stronger."

They switched out their coffee for whiskey.

"Has there ever been a moment when you felt you were there with the wolf at the same time?"

"Just once. But it was also a time I would rather forget."

"Why is that."

"Because I ate someone."

"Big whoop. I'm sure they deserved it."

Juliette swallowed hard and stared at Ruby with wide eyes. "Have you ever eaten someone?"

"Oh honey. It's not if, it's when was the last time."

"So, what exactly are you? I mean I love you to death, but this is all very new for me."

"I'm not sure I could explain exactly what I am. Other than a true badass." Ruby winked and slugged the last of her whiskey while prepping the bottle to pour another.

"Could you try?" Juliette craved kinship. She needed Ruby to explain away her freakish bits and give her a way to move through the world with a bit more optimism.

"How bout I tell you a story."

32

Once upon a time there was a girl. She lived in a beautiful land with her father. They grew herbs and raised animals and were looked to in their village for tinctures, poultices, and remedies of all sorts.

One day, a neighboring clan approached the village elders to blend the two factions to grow their strength and solidify their futures together. This was a good plan and a good deal for both, so it made sense to the elders to move forward.

The time came when the arrangement would be made official. The village gathered goods and wares from throughout both their territories to celebrate the joining. A grand party was planned with food and dancing and merriment to include their new partners.

The girl and her father were very excited for the coming arrangements. They gathered all their best recipes and potions to present a basket of goods to the visiting dignitaries as a gift. The girl and her father arrived in time to greet all their friends from the market and the village. The townsfolk banded together to prepare the great hall.

Word came that the visitors were near but that the villagers should feel free to start their party without them. The fires were stoked, food was distributed throughout the hall and the music was struck. Any dissent there might have been towards the idea of the joining had been quashed well before this date, making all who were present happy and excited for their new friends to arrive.

Outside the bustling hall, the guests arrived along with the cold fog of dusk. They stood in silence listening as the party was in full swing, ensuring that all the villagers were present. When they were assured of this, they entered.

They were greeted with warmth and open arms. They returned the greeting with a bloodbath. The villagers were slaughtered in cold blood. Shot down with crossbows. Run through with swords. Desecrated again and again all in the name of progress for the other clan.

The girl barely escaped as her father fought off the soldiers, but as she fled, a bowman of the rival clan shot her down.

You might think that would be the end of her, but she survived. She was found the next day by scavengers and brought to another village's healer. The old woman took pity on her and pulled her back from the brink of death.

As she nursed her back, the healer began to build on the girl's knowledge of herbs and potions. She taught her darker spells and incantations of shapeshifting. The girl grew adept at these spells and at the crafting of more intricate potions.

As a reward, the healer told the girl where to find the leader of the clan that killed her father and her people. She asked the old woman why she would give her such knowledge. She admitted that it was partly out of her own need for revenge and partly out of her growing love of the girl she rescued.

They devised a plan to have the girl brought to the leader as a gift. She would be presented to them as part of his stock of child bearers. The girl was to present her wares to the leader, then perform a ritual that would not only kill him, but that would run through his entire bloodline, cursing and killing all that were involved in the massacre of her people.

But there was a catch. If the girl was to perform such a rite, it would do unspeakable damage to her body and her soul. She would most likely live for an inordinate amount of time, cursed to feed on those that feed at night in order to maintain her powers and her youthful appearance.

To the girl there was no question. She would kill the man no matter the sacrifice. This was okay to her since she only lived by the sacrifice of others. She owed them this.

Word was sent to the wicked ruler and preparations were made for the girl to perform her rite. She and her healing savior worked day and night compiling the necessary ingredients, memorizing the casting words, and preparing her for the task at hand.

The day arrived for the girl to leave with the clan's guard. She and her healer prepared her baggage with the necessary elements, and she was off. They each shed one single tear at the departure of the other, for they knew that no matter what happened, it was likely the old woman would be killed, and very likely that the girl as well.

The girl arrived at the keep of the cruel clan leader. She was bathed and readied for her duties. She had a single vial to conceal that fit just behind her head, underneath her hair, secured with a bit of string.

She would need to be close to cast the spell and to get him to ingest the tincture. The only way to do this was by partaking in his lustful desires. Her sacrifice was more than she had expected, but she maintained her focus and at the right moment, under her breath, she recited the words while perched atop the man. As he writhed beneath her, she spoke the words. As she spoke the final syllables, she reached up behind her head, plucked the tincture free, and shoved it into the man's mouth, vial and all.

He tried to stop her, but she was quick and kicked him in

the chin, shattering the vial and spilling its contents down his throat.

As much as the girl had believed the healer, part of her did not believe what she was told about the consequences behind casting such a spell.

In their preparations, the girl had been given a secret route out of the keep. She gathered her clothes and any riches she could find inside the leader's chamber. It was not much, but enough to get her out of the province.

She made her way through the winding hallways and the labyrinthine waste tunnels. She exited the keep near the docks hosting a myriad of floating craft. After some bartering, she made her way onto a ship that was bound for the new world. It was an expansive place anyone could get lost in.

She was at sea for two days and two nights when she began to feel something. She couldn't explain the sensations she felt, just that it was wrong. She had been told of feelings that women have when they are with child, but that was not how she felt. She felt as if her insides were being rearranged.

In the early hours of her fifth day at sea, after taking leave of the other guests and crew for feeling ill, she was in her cabin when it happened. She heard a faint drip, then she slipped on a small blotch of blood. She noticed that the blood was dropping from her own fingertips. She screamed, but as she did, she felt her face tear. She went to the mirror. Her face had indeed torn at the corners of the mouth. A gruesome smile emerged that stretched from ear to ear. As she cried, the dainty mouth she was accustomed to, stretched wide along the tears, revealing a baroque smile of torn flesh and crooked teeth. Her fingers ached as razor-like talons pressed out from the flesh of her fingertips. She felt herself grow. She hit her head on the ceiling of her cabin. Her knees pushed backwards like a cat's hind legs. She hazarded another look in the mirror to see her eyes had changed from deep emerald to glossy black orbs. Her hair had gone from a full head of red curls to an unmanageable mane of wildly flailing fiery red locks.

She tried to cry out, and a whipping tendril-like tongue sliced the mirror in half. She had been successful in her spell and now paid the price of a thousand deaths. She was the literal monster that made men quake in their sleep.

She remained in her cabin for the rest of the trip, feeding on the stray rat that wandered by, or the sea bird that ventured too close to her porthole. As they neared land, she sped through the ship and jumped overboard to swim to shore.

In the following years, the girl learned to control her newfound gifts and was able to unlock the final piece of the healer's riddle about her power. The feeding on vampires. Her first kill was by chance as she had been stalked by a night walker, only to turn the tables and feast on his heart.

Soon she learned that by keeping their teeth, she could feed from their essence for longer periods of time as well as regain and maintain her human form. As she grew stronger, so did her ability to maintain her looks by feeding on humans instead of vampires. But it was never the same and never lasted as long.

From there she spent the coming decades and centuries feeding on vampires and developing a taste for bloodlust, thus carving out her space to be a part of the human existence once again.

And she lived ever after. But not necessarily happily.

* * *

"Wait, you're how old?"

"That's what you took from that? Really?" Ruby downed the last of the whiskey and threw the bottle into the fire. "You rest up. We have a long night ahead of us."

Ruby got up, set her empty glass on the table and walked out the door.

33

Juliette spent the day resting while Ruby wandered the forest gathering wood for the fire and enjoying the warm spring air. She returned near dusk having spent the day building her anticipation for the night's activities.

She entered the cabin and woke Juliette from her dozing.

"What's the matter? What time is it?"

Ruby smiled, caressed Juliette's cheek and leaned down for a gentle kiss.

"It's time to get up and play, my love." She kissed her and pulled Juliette up.

Juliette grasped her sheet, clinging to it to stave off the gentle chill in the cabin that threatened to pull forth the goose flesh on her naked body.

"I'm not sure this is such a good idea."

"The best ideas rarely are." Ruby grasped her hand and led her out of the dimming room and out to the forest where the day was ceding to the evening shadows that streaked across the forest floor.

Ruby let Juliette's hand drop and walked forward to where the cow was munching on its evening meal of soft grass and moss.

Ruby stroked the short hair on its neck. The cow had

escaped mealtime the night before, but even Ruby had to admit she was feeling a bit peckish.

"I hate this part."

"Top of the food chain, honey."

"What are we doing exactly?"

"Well, we, meaning me and your other self, need to break bread together. Or in this case Holstein. I have a theory."

"What's that?"

"That you are in there the whole time, you are just too scared to come out."

"So, making me observe a feeding frenzy is supposed to make me come forward?"

"Sort of. It's more that when the beast is angry and scared, it scares you. If we can calm it somehow, it might allow you to join the party and maybe even have some control over what happens when you are the wolf."

"Why would I want control over the wolf?"

"Wouldn't it be nice if you didn't have to make this kind of mountainous trek once a month? What if you could maintain a hold on the beast so that when it isn't necessary to go berserk, you don't have to."

"So, it's necessary to go berserk sometimes."

"You have no idea. Listen, I was able to subdue you last night. I'm pretty sure I can do it again."

"So, you are just gonna stand there while I eat the cow?"

"Nope, we are going to dine together. The wolf is an animal. It needs to figure out the line of dominance. Obviously, I'm the alpha, but it needs to understand that you are in power as well. So, we provide a safe environment, food, and see what happens."

Juliette was nervous but willing to give it a try. "And all we are gonna do is eat together."

"Don't put limitations on me yet. Who knows where the night will take us?" Ruby winked and Juliette chuckled.

"Looks like the sun is going to be going down very soon, so let's get ready." Ruby began to unbutton her clothes.

"I thought we were just gonna eat."

"We are, but I don't want to shred another outfit. I didn't exactly pack for that type of contingency."

"I'm just glad we are close to the same size, or I'd be nude all day long."

"There are worse things!"

34

Ruby stood by as Juliette's transformation took hold. Like the night before, Ruby watched her friend consumed by the territorial posturing of the wolf. Ruby steadied the nervous cow. As Juliette's transformation concluded, she spun toward Ruby and the cow.

Juliette's hackles raised as her playmate from the night before wickedly grinned at her. Ruby lowered her head. She exploded into her more vicious features, hair alive as if infested with angry serpents. Her eyes sprung open to reveal the onyx ovals of her demon-like persona. Her smile stretched ear to ear, a shimmer of saliva trickling down her chin. She stood tall enough to almost look Juliette's wolf in the eyes, and her talons sang as they sprang forth from her fingertips.

Juliette's snout crinkled as a low growl rumbled from her throat, and she bared her teeth, snapping at the empty air between them.

"I'm not here to fight, deary." Ruby said, the words weaving past her serpentine tongue and yellowed teeth. "I'm here to make a truce." She stroked the neck of the trembling cow that nervously stomped in between the two creatures. "You look hungry." Ruby took a step back, gesturing that she would not interfere if the wolf wanted to have the first bite.

A look of confusion washed over the wolf's face and its head cocked gently sideways. Its instinct to feed was strong, but after the failed battle the night before, it was cautious as to Ruby's intentions. A sharp bark shook the trees, and the cow gave a start.

"No need to be nervous. We could both use a bite. Don't you agree?"

The wolf's growl slowed, and its snarl calmed smoothing its curled lips to settle back down around its saliva-coated fangs. It gave a look down at the cow. Its thick tongue snaked between its lips, wetting them from side to side.

"That's it. Dinner time." Ruby grinned as the beast's hunger won out over its anger.

The wolf reared back and gave a clear howl as the moon peeked through the forested cover above them. Its cry died off and it lunged forward, collapsing the cow's throat with the heavy chomp of its jaws. The animal struggled but jaws held like a vice.

Ruby smiled and approached. The wolf's wild eyes looked at her and a gurgled snarl rumbled in its throat. "Now, now. You have to share." The wolf held tight, not willing to let go of its kill in the final moments of life. Ruby traced a single talon across the spine of the frantic bovine. She ran the finger back up to the neck and stopped next to where the wolf's fangs were sunk into the animal. Ruby opened her hand and slowly pressed her talons into the neck, just below the wolf's grip. She closed her fist around the cow's spine and with a single yank, tore it loose from the animal from the base of the skull to the tail. The cow's legs gave out as the life left its body.

The wolf postured for dominance to have the best bites, but Ruby stood tall above her swinging the bloody pendulum of the cow's spine in a hypnotic pattern. "Wanna play fetch, or just eat?" The wolf gave an annoyed yip and dove into the carcass. "Don't hog it all."

The two of them stripped the cow of its flesh and divvied up the tastiest of bites. By the end of the meal, they were bloody and bloated from the feast. They lay panting next to the meager remains. Ruby stroked the muscled neck of the wolf as it grumbled its approval and nuzzled her neck.

They lay basking in the moonlight and the meal, the feast-induced lethargy waning as they recuperated from the banquet. Juliette gently lapped at the drying droplets of the cow's remains from Ruby's chin and neck. The soft, thick tongue pulling the sticky remnants from Ruby's skin. A smile stretched across Ruby's face. With each cleansing lick, Ruby tightened her grip, pulling taut the fur that lined Juliette's neck. Juliette chuffed her approval and continued her affectionate bathing.

The forest came alive with their carnal dance, the two beasts languishing in each other's grip, teasing and tasting each other, their bestial silhouettes illuminated by the cold glow of the full moon, streaking through the outstretched arms of the leafy trees above.

They enjoyed each other until the moon made its play for the horizon and the warming glow of dawn peaked above the horizon. Ruby reverted to her human form first, holding tight to Juliette as she morphed from beast to woman. The thick coat that had sprung up the night before retreated, slipping through Ruby's grip, replaced with the gentle slick of sweat on bare skin. Juliette shivered as the chill of the morning air nipped at her skin, raising goose flesh across her body.

"Well, that was new." Juliette panted. She was exhausted and exhilarated at once. Her fingers traced intricate swirls across Ruby's arched back and the two wrapped their arms around each other searching for the heat of the other to chase the morning breeze away.

"What do you remember?" Ruby asked.

"More than usual. The night kinda swirls together. It's hard to know what happened when, but I feel so much more about my experiences than before."

"So, you were a part of the beast's world, then?"

"I think so. It was still like sitting in the back of a carriage watching the scenery float by, but this time, the roof was off, and I felt if I had a request the driver would listen."

"Oh, the driver listened for sure." Ruby purred.

Juliette giggled and gave a playful slap to Ruby's bottom. "Behave. I have no idea what last night meant, but I appreciate your efforts to help me cope with all of this. I didn't hurt you at all, did I?"

"It's cute of you to ask. Its gonna take more than a night long playful romp to hurt me, my dear."

Juliette tensed a bit, working to piece together the wild images that raced through her mind from the night before. "I didn't bite you, did I?"

"Not hard enough for me to enjoy it."

"I'm serious."

"Honestly, my dear. I doubt you could change me much further than I already am." Ruby stroked Juliette's hair to reassure her that the world was still right side up, no matter how abstract it appeared to be. "But that does bring up a good question about our friend, Brother Thomas."

Juliette went cold. She had acted so rashly when she bit him. She didn't think about what might happen, probably because she was human when he attacked her. But that would explain so much. She had changed him. She was responsible for whatever abomination he had now become. He was dangerous before as the local holder of secrets and driving force behind the town's zealots. She pressed away from Ruby to look her in the eyes. "Do you think he would change anyone?"

"Well, that would explain his recent brazenness when confronting me and the rest of the town."

"Jesus! How many more would he enlist?"

"That mad man?" Ruby's blood ran cold at the thought. She didn't worry about being recruited, but she began to imagine a world where that thin-haired, yellow-toothed plague of a man recruited far and wide to build a pack and the far-reaching damage he could reap on not only her food supply but the human race in general. "Yeah, that could be bad. I might have to look into this."

The two women rose. Juliette scanned frantically for their clothes, feeling more naked than she ever had before.

Ruby grabbed Juliette's shoulders and gave her a gentle shake to focus her panic towards her. "Juliette!"

Juliette stopped searching and locked eyes with ruby. "What?"

"Panicking is not going to do us any good."

"But—"

"But nothing. I've dealt with bad situations before and obviously can handle myself, would you agree?"

Juliette just stood rigid in Ruby's grip.

"Do you agree?" Ruby's voice was cold and confident as she stared into Juliette's scared eyes.

"I guess. How do we deal with this, though? We don't even know if he's recruiting, let alone in what numbers."

"I guess it's time to do some prying, then. So, is there anything I should know about your condition? Any other surprises, or possibly weaknesses we might need to exploit with our dear man of the cloth?"

"The only thing I remember is how I got this way and the way I killed the one that turned me."

"So, it would seem you may heal fast, but if we do enough damage to the brain or at least take the head off we might have a chance."

35

The walk back to town was quick, downhill most of the way, and both women had purpose behind their gait.

Ruby had been going over Juliette's condition and how it had probably affected the Preacher. Juliette was pragmatic and had the "greater good" in her mind when she took her sojourns into the hills to hide her beast. The preacher would not be so thoughtful. Ruby enjoyed the ruckus tumble with Juliette. The beast let her cut loose and lose control in all the right ways. Thomas would surely use his new powers to enslave his followers and possibly overrun the town or worse.

Ruby had her qualms with the world, but she liked it as it was. Having it overrun with ill-tempered wolf-folk was not a world she wanted to walk in.

"We can't let him live." Juliette stated flatly.

"No, we can't. Glad we're on the same page." Ruby took Juliette's hand in hers and the two quickened their steps.

"What are we gonna do?"

"We're gonna finish what you started with him and cut him off before he takes this too far."

"What if he's turned all of them already? What will we do?"

"We'll burn the whole damn town to the ground, one diseased pup at a time. But we're gonna need some help."

"Who would help us?"

"I have an idea."

36

They arrived back in town and made straight for Hank's. Ruby wanted to get cleaned up before talking with Ashe and they could both use a change of clothes. The town was bustling with fresh faces and the outskirts were showing signs of an influx of people with canvas tents of all sizes being erected.

They made their way through the crowds and pushed into Hank's. They stopped as they crossed the threshold. Brother Thomas stood at the bar, wagging his chin at Hank who wore an unimpressed scowl as he mindlessly cleaned glasses, trying to ignore the blather. Brother Thomas waved his arms around, as if conducting an orchestra. Ruby and Juliette's eyes were drawn to the bulky bandage around his hand covering the missing fingers Juliette had alleviated him of just the other day.

The Preacher and his entourage turned to face the somewhat disheveled pair of women who stood half in and half out of the door. "Just who we were looking for. Won't you two join us?" Brother Thomas cooed; his arms stretched wide, inviting them into his reach.

"I think we have had enough of you to last a lifetime." Ruby said.

"Oh, come now. You're not still upset about the misunderstanding between Miss Juliette and me the other day, are you? The good Lord says to turn the other cheek and forgive thy neighbor, and I have certainly done that for her."

"Go to hell, you hypocrite!" Juliette quivered with anger, staring into the cold black eyes of the elder man.

"Such language from a delicate child of God such as yourself. You really should join us for services more often so you can pave the way for your soul to enter the kingdom. Although, I'm pretty sure the likes of you will be turned away." He tipped his head forward, a wide grin stretched across his face, and his pupils engulfing much of the space in his eyes.

"I think it's time for you to leave, preacher." Hank said, his fingers grazing the body of the double barrel shotgun beneath his bar in anticipation of the possible eruption of violence that bubbled under the surface of the contentious conversation.

"Right said, brother Hank. Right said." Thomas raised his head tall, and his arms lowered to his sides. His lackeys bristled but remained in check, like good dogs.

"Come, my brethren. We have tried to reason with the apostates enough for today. They will all join us eventually in the kingdom of light." His cadence shifted from menacing to sermon-like. "For the kingdom is great and those that follow us shall feed on the manna of heaven while those that forsake us…" He stared a dark glare made all the more menacing for the wide smile he held, "shall eat of the dirt of the earth and perish at the hands of the soldiers of God."

"Amen!" his followers barked in unison. They filed in behind Thomas as he made his way towards the door.

Ruby and Juliette stepped aside as the preacher and his pack exited Hank's.

"What the fuck was that, Ruby?" Hank asked, his hands

back to cleaning glasses.

"I'll tell ya later. Have you seen Ashe today?"

"He was out earlier but I think he is back in his room now."

"Great! Hank, can you have a couple baths drawn for Juliette and me?"

Hank nodded and put his helpers into action to set up the baths.

Ruby turned to Juliette. "I want you to stay in your room till I come and get you. Can you do that form me, hon?"

"Sure. What are you gonna do?"

"Recruit."

Time to Fight

37

Ruby, fresh from her bath knocked on Ashe's door. The door unlocked and he peered out. "Ruby?"

"Hey, darlin', you up for a little company?"

He opened the door further to see Ruby, her wild red hair bunched up and slightly damp upon her head and wrapped in the comforter from her bed. "I could indulge."

She pushed her way into the room, the comforter dropping to the floor. Her naked body glistened from the bath as she worked her way around the room and lay on his bed. He scooped up the discarded blanket from the doorway as he shut away the prying eyes of the saloon from their activities.

"I'm sorry to disturb you. I'm sure if you have business to attend to, I can just entertain myself for a while." She crooned as she traced the tips of her fingers up and down her naked body, goose flesh rising in the chill of the room.

"My knitting can wait till later I guess." His warm baritone voice tickled Ruby's ears.

He made his way over to the bed and leaned down for a soft warm kiss. He moved his kisses down her neck, teasing her with gentle flicks of his tongue as he retraced the same paths her fingers had just visited.

Ruby purred, aching for his touch. She let him move down

her body, warming her skin with his kisses and priming her for the coming activities. She worked her hands down his chest unbuttoning his linen shirt and unfastening his belt. He raised up and stripped the garments from his body and lay next to her as they let each other explore the landscapes of their bodies further.

* * *

Ruby writhed, candlelight dancing across her naked curves. Her fiery red mane draped across her shoulders, tracing thin lines in the perspiration beading on Ashe's chest. Their carnal dance was in its final throes, having teased and pleased each other for the past hour. Ashe ran his fingers up Ruby's thighs and around to her back as he sat up, cradling her as she wrapped her legs around his waist.

Their eyes locked as their swaying movements synced with their intention towards climax. They clung tight as their rhythm increased in intensity, the room filling with moans and grunts coaxed from them with each thrust. The two howled as their combined motion sent wave after wave of electricity through them. Their bodies tensed, all but merging their naked selves into one as their passion ebbed slowly through their extremities.

They rolled to the side, their bodies reluctant to part, their hot skin gently clinging then releasing as they lay next to each other in the warm glow of candlelight.

The window burst open, shards of glass shooting into the room. Ashe flung two large pillows from under their heads towards the projectiles, absorbing the sharp glass as the pillows erupted into a storm of fluffy feathers. Ruby rolled off the bed, landing on all fours, furious that her fun had been interrupted.

Ashe rolled off the other side, snatching up the pistol he

had laid on the nightstand and pulling back the hammer in a fluid motion.

The room shook with the heavy footsteps of the eight-foot wolf that stomped around the room. Its jaws snapped at the feathers that lilted through the air. Each chomp sounded like the crack of a whip. It swung its arms and shook its head, attempting to clear the air of the fluffy obstructions so it could lock in on its prey.

Ashe stood tall, his naked silhouette stretched across the bed and floor between him and the monster. He fired shot after shot with deadly accuracy into the beast's chest. Fur and ragged tissue exploded off the wolf with each impact but healed almost as quick. His weapon clicked empty. The feathery impediment cleared, and the beast turned towards him. Its snout curled into a wicked smile as it stretched across the sharp fangs that glistened, eager to sink themselves into the naked man and Ruby.

"Ruby! Run!" he yelled as he whipped the pistol's chamber free from the barrel to unload the empty casings. His eyes widened as he looked to Ruby's side of the bed and instead of the soft, warm curves he had indulged in moments before, he saw Ruby crouched on her side of the bed, her inner self springing into action.

He stood agape watching her leap forward. She slammed into the side of the wolf, pinning it to the wall. She and the wolf slashed at each other, each wound healing almost as quickly as it opened. The wolf snapped at her, confusing her wild hair for her head and chomping into her tresses as she whipped her head up, slamming into the bottom of its jaw and chipping a couple of its massive teeth. The tooth pieces tinkled to the ground with a sound similar to Ashe's spent casings. Ruby drove her talons into either side of the wolf's rib cage and held tight. The wolf roared in pain.

Ruby turned her grotesque face toward Ashe, "Time to

reload, lover!"

It was a shock to see her stretched smile and mouth filled with rows of teeth, but it jarred him back to the present. He lunged for the chair where his gun belt hung. He plucked six fresh shells from it and reloaded with lightning speed. He flicked his wrist, and the six-shooter snapped back in place, waiting for him to prime the hammer. "Ruby! Get out of there!"

Ashe brought his pistol to bear on the wolf's head. Ruby clenched her fists, snapping ribs and tearing into the animal's organs as she pulled down and dropped to the floor to clear the way for his shot. "Do it!"

Ashe emptied his gun into the animal's skull. The wall and ceiling darkened with brain matter and mated fur. It slumped against the wall and slid down to the floor, its hole-riddled head settling next to Ruby.

The room was quiet except for Ashe and Ruby's heavy breathing. Ruby was getting up when the wolf swatted her across the room, its disfigured head regrowing as Ashe watched in awe.

Ruby righted herself. "Fuck this bitch!" She tromped to the beast's wriggling body, leaned down and opened her maw. She chomped down on the wolf's thick neck and worked her jaws, sawing through muscle and tendons. The pop of cartilage and bone crackled through the room. Within seconds, she was through the spine, and had ripped the head clean from the body. She spat it across the room. It hit the ground with a heavy thud. The wolf's body went limp.

Ashe walked up next to Ruby and they both watched as the wolf regressed back into its human form. "I guess there is more than one way to skin a wolf." Ruby said, her more feminine shape and soft face colored by the animal's blood looked up into Ashe's astonished eyes.

38

They stood for a second taking in the gruesome scene of the young, naked man that lay headless on Ashe's floor. Ashe turned his gaze to his blood-coated bed partner. Shock settled in, pushing the rush of adrenaline aside. His knees wobbled under his weight. He stumbled to the chair and flopped down. Making love with Ruby would have been enough to do this, but add the horror show he had just witnessed, and he was more than spent.

From outside the window came a repetitive smack. It was a single person applauding down on the street. Ruby walked to the window and glared down at Brother Thomas, a wide malevolent grin taunting her from below. His bandage strewn on the ground at his feet, his freshly grown fingers on display as he clapped. "I'll see you soon, Jezebel!" His grin went cold, and he turned and walked away into the night.

Ruby turned back to Ashe. He sat dumbstruck in the chair, staring at the headless body at the foot of the bed. His gun dangled from the tips of his fingers and sweat gathered in a slick layer on his body.

"Nice moves, lover." Ruby cooed as she swiped her forearm across her lips to clear away some of the gore left from her killing bite.

They both turned to the door with a start as Hank franticly pounded on the door threatening to break down the sturdy oak barrier.

"What do we do?" Ashe asked, shaken by what he had witnessed.

"We should probably let them in before they break the door down." Ruby was draped in a silk robe. "You might want to pull on your pants, though. I don't mind the view, but I'm not sure how shy you are in crowded situations." She winked, trying to lighten the mood.

Ashe let his pistol drop to the floor. He rose up and grabbed his pants. Ruby opened the door as his trousers cleared his hips, hiding away the gifts that God gave him.

Hank stood there, a panicked look on his face, along with a half dressed and still damp Juliette and a couple of Hank's more loyal customers. "What the hell is going on up here?"

"Hell's about right, Hank." Ruby said.

Hank looked past her to see the naked headless body on the floor a growing pool of blood oozing out of its neck hole. "Who's supposed to clean this up?" he asked.

"Before we get too far into this, I'm pretty sure that thing over there is not coming back, but to be safe, we should probably cart it off to the burn pile to make sure."

Everyone stood unmoving, working to process what Ruby said.

"Seriously, its bad to let these things have time to heal in case I didn't take care of it the first time."

"Jesus, I need better tenants." Hank said. He turned to his friends, "Go get the wheelbarrow and do as the lady says."

As he turned to go, Ruby grasped Hank's arm. "Hank?"

"What is it, Ruby?" He sighed as he asked, certain he didn't really want to know.

"Do you trust your boys?" She gave a nod to the two men fighting back the urge to vomit.

"As much as I trust anyone, I suppose."

She looked in his eye and lowered her voice a bit, "We need to talk, but I want you to only bring in folks you know you can trust. Can you do that for me?"

Her sincerity took him aback. He was not used to such a tone from Ruby. "Yeah. I get it. What's going on Ruby?"

"Just come back in about an hour. Bring these two and any more you can muster that you know have your back." She nodded to him, her brows high, inquiring if he understood.

Hank patted her hand that clung to his arm. "You got it."

They smiled gently at each other. Ruby let loose his arm and he turned to head back down to the bar. "Get a move on, ya lazy saps. What's a matter? You never seen a headless body before?" He hollered over his shoulder to his helpers.

The two men ambled in and squeamishly picked up the headless, naked body. One grabbed under its shoulders, the other at its feet. Ruby walked across the room and plucked up the head as they were almost out the door. "Don't forget this." She dropped the misshapen cranium on the dead man's stomach. The worker lifting the shoulders couldn't hold it any longer and spewed the contents of his stomach, dowsing the headless body with partially digested roast beef and potatoes. He managed to keep a hold of the body, and his friend managed not to lose his lunch.

"Oh, hell, Leroy. Can't you wait till we're outside to do that?"

39

The two lackeys made their way out of the room and down the stairs but not before Ruby managed to arrange a blanket over the dead body.

Ruby closed the door and looked to her two friends. Juliette and Ashe, both in varying degrees of disheveled undress looked at her with vacant eyes. Ashe kept his distance from her, still a bit shaken having seen her true form bite the head off a werewolf just minutes ago.

"What are we gonna do, Ruby?" Juliette said, fiddling with the thin cotton top that clung to her damp skin.

"I'm getting the fuck out of town, that's what I'm doing." Ashe shook himself out of his shock and frantically searched his room for the rest of his clothes that had been tossed around during their lovemaking.

"We're going to stop that maniac, that's what."

"Are you totally insane?" Ashe said. "I'm just as worried about you as that freak downstairs. I mean, what the hell was that? What the hell are YOU? And where's my fucking boot?" He dashed through the room on the hunt for his belongings, tossing them towards his saddle bags to pack or throwing on clothes.

"You need to settle down, lover."

"Settle down?" He stopped mid-toss and stared at her. "Settle down? You just bit the head off a goddamned giant wolf."

"Would you rather I let him rip us apart? Because that is what he was sent up here to do."

"And why was that, exactly? What have you gotten me into here? I'm just here to collect my bounty and blow off some steam. I never signed on for this."

"You're being dramatic." Ruby brushed off his comments and let her silk robe drop to the ground. She walked naked over to the dresser and plucked a white button-down shirt from his drawer. She pulled on the linen garment and buttoned it up.

"Please, Ruby," Juliette said as she buttoned her top and straightened her skirt. "He's not exactly wrong. What is going on here?"

"Well, my love, since your encounter with our preacher friend down there, he seems to have inherited your primal traits."

"Jesus! You're one of those too?" Ashe threw his hands up in the air in frustration and continued to haphazardly pack.

"Technically, yes, but I don't want to hurt anyone."

"Well, they didn't get the memo about reining in their appetite, now did they."

"Be nice." Ruby chided, "This is not *really* Juliette's fault. She was only standing up to that hypocrite. I would have done the same." Ruby put her hand on Juliette's cheek and gave her a warm look. "It's not her fault that her bite had side effects." She blew a kiss at Juliette, who blushed and pulled away with a coy glance.

"Jesus! You're both crazy. I mean, I've seen some shit but this takes the cake. And frankly, I'm not exactly equipped to deal with this."

Ruby turned to him, "No, you're not. But you are one of

the most capable men I have come across in a long time, so why don't you quit your bitching and sit down for a moment so we can talk this through." She pointed to the bed and motioned for him to take a seat next to Juliette. "Here, I'll sit over here even." She said mockingly and sat down in the chair next to the wash basin.

Ashe huffed and looked back and forth from Ruby, to Juliette, to his saddle bags and back around the room. He gave up. His head fell and he skulked over to the bed and sat next to Juliette.

"There. That's better. Let me start by saying that this is a bit outside my comfort zone."

"*Your* comfort zone?" the bounty hunter sneered.

"Yes. I don't play well with others usually. I prefer to be on my own and tend to let these situations run their course while I'm on the way out of town. Just like you tried to do just now." She looked at him and he softened slightly.

"In fact, it was not too long ago that I found myself in a similar situation that the preacher is in. I had a town eating out of my hand and then it bit me, so I tried to destroy it."

"How'd that work out for you?"

"Not great." Ruby sounded regretful at the mention of the incident at Thrawl and the Braided Pony. "But that doesn't matter. That was then, this is now. I see what I did before was, let's say, misguided.

"The real point is that this asshole masquerading as a holy man is more toxic than I could have ever been, even before he was a wolf. He has an agenda that involves more than just satisfying his selfish desires." She was fascinated by her revelations. Ruby never thought of herself as reflective. Her moral evolution stopped the day she transformed into the creature. But wanting to help these people in front of her, let alone this town, left her curious about what had happened to her after facing defeat back in Thrawl.

"The point here is that that madman would set the entire world on fire just for the fun of it and even at my worst I never indulged such apocalyptic tenets." She looked up from her fidgeting fingers and into the eyes of Juliette and Ashe. "He has to be stopped, and I truly believe that we are the only ones that can make that happen."

"Just us?" Juliette said, a nervous quiver in her voice.

"Oh, God no! We're gonna get Hank and his friends to help too. We're gonna need some cannon fodder, I mean muscle." She gave a nervous smile. "The hard part is gonna be convincing Hank to give up the profits on all the moonshine we're gonna need."

40

Hank returned to the room an hour later, five cronies in tow. Ruby and Ashe used the bedding to clean up the rest of the blood so the new visitors wouldn't slip as they came to hear Ruby detail her plan. She had already explained things to Ashe and Juliette, and now it was time to convince the new recruits that she was not crazy and that fighting alongside her was a better option than bowing down to the preacher.

"We good so far, Hank?" Ruby asked as they filed into the room.

"All square. No one is gonna go looking for that body any time soon."

"Okay. I know Hank trusts you all, so I'm gonna do the same." She looked intensely into the eyes of each of the newcomers.

"Yeah, so what's this all about?" Jethro asked, annoyed to be pulled away from his evening activities.

"It's about your life and the lives of everyone else in the town."

Hank and his friends all sniggered a bit at Ruby's hyperbolic statement. "Okay, lady." Jethro turned to Hank, "I'm gonna get back to Suzie. I got a bonus this week and I'm eager to see if she'll finally suck on my knob." He turned towards the door. He placed his hand on the handle and was surprised by the clawed grip that closed over it.

"Holy hell!" He yelped looking into Ruby's wild, onyx eyes.

"I'm gonna ask nice that you hear me out before you run off to Suzie. Between you and me, she enjoys a man's fingers, and I would hate to relieve you of yours. What do you say, big guy?" Her comment was accented by a flick of her tendril-like tongue on the tip of his nose.

"Yes, ma'am." He trembled, glancing Ruby's widened smile.

Ruby let go and he pulled his hand back and rubbed at it to make sure all his digits were intact.

Ruby shifted back to her human form. "Alright. I know what I am about to tell you will sound… let's say, far-fetched. But hopefully my little demonstration has at least given you a hint of the less-than-ordinary circumstances we will be delving into here. Yes?"

The group nodded. The big man nodded with enthusiasm.

"What we have here is a holy man that believes he is God. He's decided to recreate the world in his image."

"What kind of riddle are you weaving, Ruby?" Hank asked.

"The kind of riddle that ends in a lot of bloodshed. And I'm sorry to say Hank, a lot of wasted whiskey."

Hank's eyes went wide.

Ruby laid out the situation, explaining how Brother Thomas had been infected and how, with his natural penchant for control, he had been turning his congregants into his pack. It had become apparent, with his brazen attack on Ruby and Ashe, that he was not interested in slowing the infection rate of his congregation. He was, in fact, raising the stakes and this might be their only opportunity to rid this town of him and his followers before he set his sights beyond the borders of Dry Bed.

"You really believe he's doin' all this?" Hank asked.

"I know he is. I've seen his kind before, and they are not interested in moderation when it comes to power."

"Just when things were starting to pick up in this town, too." Hank shook his head then turned to everyone. "Who's in the mood for a late-night revival?"

41

The group wove through the dusty streets to the church. There was little activity this time of night on a Sunday as the rail workers were already tucked away to rest and the townsfolk were at home with their families. The posse were armed with whiskey jugs and whatever weaponry they could carry. The alcohol sloshed at their sides as they gathered at the bottom of the church steps.

Ashe stared up at the stark white façade. "Not gonna sugarcoat this. It's gonna get messy tonight. I'm here to put down some naughty mutts. I'd prefer not to bury any of you. Everyone clear on that?"

The group nodded as Ruby glanced around. "That's fine. It's less efficient, but fine. Me and Hank are gonna go in and make sure that there aren't any non-converts inside. Don't want to cook up anyone not walking on all fours. While we do that, you all give this church a fresh coat of moonshine. Just please don't light it till we come out. I had a bad experience with fire and I'm not looking to repeat." She smiled as the posse acknowledged their task.

"Remember, if you come across any of his true followers, don't waste any time."

"What do you mean?" Jethro asked, head tilted.

"I mean take their head off and light 'em on fire. Think you can handle that, big guy?"

He nodded sheepishly as she gave him a condescending pat on the cheek.

Ruby started toward the steps. Juliette grabbed her hand and Ruby turned to her. "You be careful in there." Her eyes were wide with concern.

"Don't worry, love. It's nothin' more than a rowdy night at the saloon. I'll be back soon." She winked at her and squeezed her hand gently.

Ruby nodded to Hank, and they went up the stairs to the doors. The pop of corks on whiskey jugs was echoed by the sharp click of Hank's sawed-off double barrel shotgun as he and Ruby climbed the chapel's steps. The rest of the group spread out to liberally anoint the sides of the church with a coat of moonshine.

42

The heavy red door of the chapel swung wide, greeting the visitors with a chorus of creeks from the rusted hinges. The room was lit by the moon pushing through the rustic stained-glass windows that stretched to the rafters.

"Charming," Ruby said.

Hank huffed, "Not exactly inviting at night, is it?"

"Honestly, I feel more at home now than when Preacher is leaning into that lectern."

The floorboards creaked under their weight but there was no other sound. Rows of pews flanked an aisle pointing to the altar and lectern where Brother Thomas would address his followers. Ruby chuckled softly at the idea of a wolf leading the sheep.

"What is it?" Hank whispered, his focus on keeping his ears open.

"It's nothing. Just something struck me as funny." Ruby scanned the surroundings, her eyes sharp as they discerned shadow from structure. The moonlight was dim and the shapes that surrounded them did not make it easy to see whether there was anything dangerous in there.

A sound out of step with them caught their attention and they stopped cold.

"You hear that?" Hank rasped, his gun trained forward.

"Shh!" Ruby scanned the spot trying to discern whether there was something there or whether the building was just shifting under their weight. She motioned to move toward the corner so they could close in on whatever it was.

Hank split off down a pew while Ruby stayed in the aisle. They approached the scuffling from two sides. They swiftly came together around the corner and stopped. A rat stole away with a communion wafer and scuttled towards the altar. Their amused gazes followed the critter.

A massive, clawed paw dropped down on the rat, flattening the little thief beneath the weight of a mass of tufted fur, claws, and fangs. The room rang with a low rattle as its lip curled up, revealing a glistening row of sharp fangs that stretched along its snout to the back of its massive jaws.

"I think they knew we were coming." Ruby said. She flicked her wrists and her elegant talons sprung out eager to make merry with the huge beast's insides.

The two slowly backed away, opening space between themselves and the drooling beast.

The door to the chapel slammed shut, startling the duo. They spun, keeping one eye on the beast at the altar and the other on the animal that had slammed and secured the door to the outside, trapping their would-be meals inside.

"You want the front or the back?" Ruby asked. A wicked grin of anticipation stretched across her lips.

"If I have a choice, I guess I'll take the rear."

"Alright, but you have to pay extra."

Hank answered her quip by emptying both barrels into the chest of the beast at the altar. Fur and blood exploded with the impact and the creature flew backwards crashing into the altar with a clatter. "Never mind. I'm fresh outta change."

The wolf at the door roared and charged but Ruby was already halfway to it. She hooked its arm in hers before it knew where she was. She pushed forward and spun the gnashing creature into the back two rows of pews. The snap of its spine bending the wrong way crackled in the air as the wolf crashed through the two splintered benches and slammed into the back corner.

The clatter of the beasts trying to regain their senses was joined by the clatter of spent shells as Hank reloaded his shotgun. "I'm not lucky enough for that to have been all, am I?"

Both creatures popped up from the ground, shaking off the daze of the initial attacks.

"What fun would that be?" Ruby said, her tone playful. "Remember, you gotta take the head off. Shooting it in the chest just pisses them off."

"Great!"

Hank stared down the growling animal behind the altar. It roared at him and swiped away the wooden fixture, splintering it against the wall as it trudged forward to face off with him again.

Hank pulled back both hammers and leveled the gun at the beast's chest. As it neared, he adjusted his aim and went for the maim instead. He lowered the barrels and as the beast was almost upon him, he fired, severing the leg from its body. The creature howled and toppled forward, its head crashing down onto the corner of a pew.

It lay motionless and bleeding. Hank moved forward and quickly emptied and reloaded. He locked the barrel back in position. He stood over the motionless animal and leveled the barrel just below the animal's skull. He pulled the trigger and evaporated the animal's neck. The floor beneath it was painted with blood and spinal fluid. The heavy head bounced away down the pew as the rest of the body slumped to the floor underneath him. He reloaded again and for good measure pressed the two barrels into the wolf's temple and fired, spraying the bench with the top half of its head, ending its life with a squelch of brain matter and skull bone.

Ruby was occupied with her playmate. They wrestled amongst the back pews, slashing and gnashing at each other with furious, primal speed. The snap of their teeth like whip cracks echoing off the walls. They locked claws and pressed forward into each other, trying to buckle the other. Ruby grinned, barely tapped into her full strength. "Nighty night, Fifi." She rasped with wicked intent.

Her tongue whipped forward with lightning speed and wrapped around the animal's neck. She yanked to the side and constricted her tongue. The werewolf's eyes went wide as its neck popped free and Ruby flung its head to the other side of the room. It bounced to a halt against the far wall, and the beast's grip went limp in her hands. She pushed the lifeless body away from her and made her way to the still-chomping head.

Hank joined her. They looked down at the macabre vision of the flopping head as it wildly chomped at nothing.

"Want to do the honors?" Ruby gestured to Hank.

He answered by locking in two fresh shells. He pressed the barrel into the mouth and squeezed the trigger, splitting it in two with a thunderous boom.

The door burst open and Ashe, both guns drawn, moved into the room. He looked to Ruby and Hank, a misting of wolf blood speckling their faces and two headless naked bodies decorating the empty chapel.

"Everything okay, you two?" He said, ready to fire.

"You missed all the fun." Ruby said, wiping at the droplets of blood congealing on her cheek.

Ashe released the hammers on both guns and holstered them. "Well, we're ready to light it up outside if you're done messin' around."

The three stepped out of the church and into the crisp

night air. As they stepped off the last step the church went up in a tower of flames. They joined the rest of the group and admired the whiskey-aided bonfire.

"Baptized in flame," Ruby said, then turned to her companions. "Now let's finish this."

"That's not all?" Jethro asked.

"Nope. We need to stop this at the source." Ruby turned to Hank. "Sorry, but we're gonna need a lot more whiskey."

"I figured. We can load up the wagon at my storage shack. How much we gonna need?"

"Enough to make them think they're already in Hell."

43

With such small numbers, they had agreed that coming at the ranch in the dark would be the best option. The six of them slowed the horses and wagon as they neared the perimeter fence. They had packed as much of Hank's raw alcohol in the back of the wagon as they could. Hank directed Conrad and Jethro to creep to the barn and quietly secure the doors on the front and back.

They'd scouted the compound for a half hour to figure where everyone was holed up. The main house only had a couple of lanterns lit but the barn was aglow with flickering light seeping out from between the planks. They heard a faint murmur emanating from inside. Most likely the sounds of yet another of Brother Thomas' bombastic sermons.

The two men skulked to the barn and secured a large plank across the door to slow the exit once the chaos began. They did the same to the back exit. They turned and scuttled back to the rest of the crew who were already prepping the alcohol for quick dispersion on the barn to ensure their fire would take in the shortest time. Surprise was key.

Hank pulled back the canvas atop the wagon. The bottles underneath gently clinked against each other. Everyone gathered, eyes wide, and mouths watering.

"This is gonna be such a waste." Ruby shook her head at the sight of so many bottles of Hank's distillate.

"You're telling me," Hank said, a little choked up with a tear visible in the corner of his good eye. "This is a month of profits we're about to burn up. This better work!"

Everyone nodded and went to work. They formed an assembly line and uncorked the bottles, then stuffed rags in the tops. They made short work of the chore. The prepped bottles were arranged around the barn in groups so that everyone could launch their attack from different locations.

With the bottles prepped and emptied from the wagon, Hank distributed unlit torches to everyone. "No going back now, folks. We can't let these beasts get away and we only have one shot at this. Aim to kill. Destroy the heads." He glanced around the circle of vigilantes gathered in the dark. He saw the gentle nods of agreement.

"And don't forget to have fun out there, kids." Ruby grinned, her inner grotesque smile creeping up the sides of her face, a twinkle of needle-like points lit by the moonlight peeked from behind her lips.

Hank pulled the cork from a small bottle and dowsed the torches. Juliette followed behind him, lighting matches and bringing the flames to life with a gentle *whomp* as each took to flame. The band of arsonists spread out and settled next to a pile of bottles along the perimeter of the barn.

Ruby found her spot. She set the torch on the ground and lit two fuses. She plucked up the bottles and looked to see that everyone was ready. She looked to her left and nodded, signaling Juliette to do the same. Then she looked right at Hank and nodded again. He nodded in turn and signaled the next person down the line.

The dark sky was lit by flickering rags flapping in the wind as bottles were launched at the barn. One after another smashed against the sides of the barn. Each impact set free the flammable contents, coating the surrounding surfaces in flaming liquid death. The dry wood of the aged barn invited the flames to feast on its bounty of fuel and after a couple of salvos the entire barn was consumed in a yellow-orange plume of flame and thick black smoke.

The screams were not immediate, but as soon as the realization that the exits were blocked came about, the crackle of flames was accompanied by the strained screams and howls of the panicked occupants.

Outside Ruby and company continued to feed the fire with bottle after bottle of accelerant. The heat from the blaze itched their skin as they stoked the growing bonfire with each subsequent lob. The doors of the barn rattled with the struggle inside. Claws scraped at the inside walls, desperate to break through to the cool air on the other side.

The band of arsons stood ready, waiting for the first beast to break through the inferno. It didn't take long. The bar across the door cracked under the weight of three hulking beasts charging the door. "Get ready!" Hank called to his companions, weapons at the ready and muscles tensed in anticipation of the horrors about to break free.

The barricade splintered and the door burst open, rocking free from its hinges and flying to the ground, creaking under the weight of the frothing beasts, a cloud of smoke wafted out of the barn behind them.

"Give em hell!" Ruby, fully transformed now, screeched while throwing two lit bottles at the creatures. Both bottles landed on the wolf to the right of center. It erupted into flames and took off yelping and swatting at its burning flesh. The fur melting away as the flames took hold in an unquenchable feast of the beast's flesh.

The lead werewolf, smoke lifting off its back, snarled at Ruby. She smiled a wicked, wide smile back at the preacher in all his wolfish glory. Her tongue whipped out of her mouth and lapped her lips, the hunger of the fight fueling her.

From behind the two wolves came a throng of animals, filing out through the smoke, coughing and chomping at the fresh air as the thick haze gave way to the frenzy of the pack. The posse let loose their arsenal of lit bottles. The night ignited with bright pops as the bottles exploded on the barn, the ground surrounding the animals, and the beasts themselves. The inferno crackled in chorus with howls, yelps and bloodthirsty yells. With the initial barrage the group was able to thin the pack considerably, but they were still outnumbered as the barn spewed forth one werewolf after another.

Flaming bottles were replaced with firearms, axes, and bladed farm implements. In the chaos of battle, it was hard to tell who had the upper hand. A wolf would go down, smoldering and slashed to pieces on the ground, only to be joined by one of the townsfolk. A head bit clean off here, an arm slashed from its body there. The grounds of the compound were riddled with human and beast parts alike.

Ruby stepped forward keeping the gaze of the man-wolf locked on her. A protective follower charged her. She spun and traced her deadly talons in a graceful pattern in the wolf's chest before plunging the hand into its chest, engulfing its heart in her iron grip and squeezing it to mush as she ripped its head clean off with the other hand. The lifeless, furry body crumpled to the ground accompanied by the thump of its head.

Brother Thomas narrowed his lupine eyes, his lips curling across his massive teeth. Ruby winked and lapped at the sour blood dripping from her claws. It was Ruby's turn. She calmly walked towards him. She took down wolf after wolf as they attempted to take her out before she reached their leader. She was evening the odds for the townsfolk who were now able to team up, two to a wolf, cutting their way through the ranks.

She stood defiantly in front of the panting beast. Anger boiled up in him as he watched his followers burned, hacked, and dismembered, the circle of townsfolk closing around Ruby and him, boxing him in between them and the burning pyre of the barn. They had started with six and had been whittled down to four, but not a single beast had survived their assault, saving the biggest for last.

"What do ya say, Preacher? Ready to meet your maker?" Ruby stood tall; her demonic lines accentuated by the flames dancing across her flesh. He winced as the barn behind him cracked and collapsed in on itself, sealing in any wolves that might still be waiting behind.

Ruby's mane billowed and snaked around her. Her lithe, muscled arms were coated in blood and clumps of matted fur. Her muscular legs, knees bent back, pulsed with anticipation of the attack. Her onyx eyes were wide and unblinking while her tongue whipped back and forth, wetting her needle-like teeth.

Unwilling to wait, one of the townsfolk charged Brother Thomas, his scythe above his head. The wolf closed the distance faster and slashed his leg away. The man fell and skidded to a halt on his back, screaming and reaching for the spurting stump. The preacher stood over the screaming man, lifted his leg and crushed the man's skull beneath his massive paw. He looked up at Ruby, a satisfied grin lifting at the corners of his snout as he raised his paw, shaking the bone and brain from between his toes.

Ruby kept his gaze. Others in the circle tensed as if about to charge. Ruby held up her hand, "He's mine!" She flicked her wrists, and her claws extended to their full length.

The two demonic gladiators charged one another. They came together and clasped hands pressing into each other, testing the other's strength as they snapped their tooth-filled maws at the air between them. They dug their claws into their opponent's hands, determined to bring the other down first. The crackle of the fire was paired with the squelch of flesh giving way. The preacher sneered at Ruby. He towered over her and pressed down with his full wight. Ruby ground her feet into the earth bracing against his heft as he forced her backwards. Ruby tensed, "Enough!" She focused her energy into her grip. She stopped skidding backward and held her ground. Her legs tensed under the strain as she raised herself up meeting the wolf eye to eye. She held tight, then dropped between the wolf's legs, spinning while maintaining her hold. The snap of bones filled the air as she used his own weight to break his forearms as she pulled him forward and down to the ground. She held tight, spun again and yanked free both of his hands. The wolf howled and writhed on the ground, staring at his bleeding stumps in disbelief.

Ruby unclasped the disembodied claws. She shook her wounded hands, and they healed almost immediately. The preacher was changing back to his human form, laughing and crying at the same time, his arms spouting forth, coating his naked body in his own blood. "I bet you feel proud of yourself tonight, don't you, Jezebel?" His sentence accented by a spurt from his arm.

"I will be soon, old man." Ruby leaned over the bleeding, cackling man. She clamped a taloned hand into his shoulder, the other she drove into his groin, piercing his pelvic bone. He screamed at the insertion. She lifted the squirming man, who was helpless against her. Her joints cracked as her knees clicked back into place. She knelt and brought the man down, snapping his spine on the point of her knee joint. His belly distended as the spine pushed forward, slicing through organs and tissue, peeking through his belly button. He spat blood, fighting to gurgle out more insults. Ruby had assumed that any injuries caused to the wolves by her would not heal as quickly as from a human, and she was right. It seemed her venom had its perks with these creatures. It may not paralyze but it still gave her a bit of an advantage.

She rolled him off her knee and he thudded to the ground. Behind them, the roof timbers of the barn gave way, and it folded in on itself. Sparks flew into the air.

The preacher rasped, puffing gusts of dry earth past his blood and mucus coated lips. More liquid than air filled his lungs as he slowly drowned in his own injuries. Ruby knelt one more time and whispered into his ear. "Time for a barbecue, Padre. Hope you like your meat well done." She sunk her talons into the nape of his neck, lifted him up and dragged him to the churning flames of the barn. She braced herself and flung his dripping body into the inferno. As he disappeared, one last scream escaped his lips.

Ruby turned back to her friends. Ashe approached her, the flicker of the fire illuminating him. "That it, then?"

Ruby, back in her human form, looked around at the scattered bodies, some of which lay shallowly breathing dying breaths. "We need to finish what we started."

"What do you mean?"

"These people will change if we don't end them now and then we just start all over."

"All of them?" His brow raised reminding, Ruby that one of their own was also a werewolf.

"I'll leave that up to her."

The two went back to the townsfolk and Juliette. They divvied up the dirty deed of dispatching the possibly-turned, along with the dying wolves that littered the compound's grounds. The night air rang with merciful gunfire as the bullets were fired into the brainpans, and then the bodies were tossed into the still roaring flames of the barn.

The gruesome task took only about an hour along with

setting the main house ablaze after looting anything of value or necessity form the interior and loading it into Hank's carriage. Regrettably, Hank had been struck by one of the wolves in the melee. Before being put down by one of the gambler's bullets, he asked that his place and treasured moonshine recipe be left to the ladies of the bar so they could maintain his legacy. The deal was sealed with a leaden stamp to his brain.

44

The ride back to town was a quiet one. Aside from Ruby, many of them had never seen such carnage. Even for Ruby something was different. She had never relied on others, especially not on humans. She had trouble reconciling her newfound appreciation for what she had always considered to be little more than a source of food or playthings. Even when she was still human, which she remembered very little of anymore, she had had little connection to those around her. Being a part of the solution was strange. Working to make others' lives better was not part of what she considered to be her core tenets. Was she now going to look at humans differently? Would she even relegate herself to seeing vampires differently? How would she feel the next time she needed to feed?

They rode the remainder of the night and welcomed the first rays of dawn as they made their way back to Hank's saloon to bring news to its new proprietors.

The band of warriors was tired. They slid from their mounts and landed with heavy feet. Folks went their separate ways, with Ruby, Ashe, and Juliette going into Hank's for fresh baths and to sleep the rest of the day away.

Ashe and Ruby shared a bath, aiding each other in

scrubbing away the grime from the night before. Soon the clean, hot water in the tub was replaced with a frothy mixture of dirt and blood. They cleaned up and pulled the plug to let the murky mixture of the previous night's horror spill away into the back alley where it drained off.

The two comforted each other, gently making love, attempting to replace the screams and visceral images that flashed through their heads. When they were done, they lay in each other's arms, panting and awaiting the blanket of sleep to wrap them up.

45

It didn't take long for the ladies of Hank's saloon to move past mourning their beloved landlord and embark on envisioning their new business. The saloon, come dusk, was business as usual with an unlikely, boisterous crowd. The railroad had been making its way towards the town for months. It made more sense for the workers and administrators to take up lodging there and they had already made themselves comfortable in Hank's along with filling the other boarding houses to capacity.

The drinks flowed, cards were dealt, and the saloon rang with the playful sounds of its strident piano. Laughter and gleeful chirps from the working girls greeted the fresh faces. They made their rounds establishing new relationships with future regulars for the coming months of railroad business.

Juliette, Ashe and Ruby settled down at a corner table near the back entrance enjoying a bottle of Hank's finest aged whiskey. Between belts, they struck up a friendly game of poker.

"Have you thought more about what you want to do, Juliette?" Ashe asked, fanning out his cards.

"I want to stay around here I think, but I'm thinking cattle might be a good business." She smiled and winked at Ruby.

"Cattle makes sense. Good money, plenty of customers with the railroads coming in. Not to mention, it's easy to replace stock when the hunger strikes." Ruby winked back.

"You really think that's wise given your... condition?" Ashe selected a card from his hand and laid it face down. He replaced it with a fresh card from the top of the deck.

"I don't have the aspirations that the good preacher did. I just want to live a quiet life and be left alone." Juliette dropped two, which Ashe replaced with a graceful flick of his wrist.

"Not sure about you two, but it might be about time for me to pull up stakes." Ruby held onto her hand. "Last town I stayed in too long, left me with a bad taste in my mouth. That and it's time to restock some of my supplies that are not so easily procured in such a bustling environment." She caressed the small pouch hanging from her neck between her thumb and forefinger, beckoning for a refill that was going to be more difficult to replenish than she wanted to think about right now.

"I've heard of a few bounties up north," Ashe said, "that can keep me occupied and fed through the winter. I'll probably be taking my leave soon, as well." He fanned out his cards displaying a full house, aces and eights. "I hope this ain't foretelling, but can anyone beat my dead man's flush?" He grinned and took a swig of whiskey.

Juliette shook her head. "Not me, pretty sure my three sevens are no good."

"It's all yours, hon." Ruby splayed out her two pairs of sixes and queens. "I guess the next bottle is on us then." Nodding to Juliette.

"I'll get it. I need to powder my nose anyway. Be right back."

Juliette pushed away from the table and made her way down the back hallway to the facilities behind the saloon.

Hank had kept not only a clean and inviting saloon, but for what it was, an outhouse that was near inhabitable. Juliette used the facilities and headed back to her friends.

A charred, clawed hand clutched her throat, lifting her so the ground was just beyond the reach of her toes. They traced figure eights in the thin dust as she gasped for air. The preacher's charred remains held her tight. His flesh still smoldering from the night before. Clumps of melting tissue dripped to the ground from his outstretched arm. Juliette grabbed at his arm, her fingers slipping along the damaged flesh and stripping blackened bits away as she clawed for freedom.

"I'm sure you and your friends think you are clever having relieved me of my pack. You should have known though that I was something a bit different." He stared at her with one eye, the other socket filled with a milky orb. Juliette stared into his mangled face, his nose askew and hanging by sticky sinew. The bone from his skull peeked through burned-away skin and muscle. Only a few strands of his wispy white hair remained, and they glistened red with gore.

Juliette gasped. She willed herself to transform but couldn't tap into her powers. Panic rose as darkness encircled her vision. The world grew distant, and even the pain from his claws piercing her soft flesh ebbed as consciousness drifted away. Her blood slipped past the yellowed claws dripping down his arm joining the congealed globules on the dusty ground below.

"Don't worry about your friends, little one. I'll make sure they are well taken care of once I'm done with you. Be sure to say hello to my brother, you unworthy welp." A grin stretched across where his lips used to be, pulling the remaining membrane taught, exposing his teeth as his snout extended forward. Canines longer than a finger sprouted fresh from empty sockets, pushing out the broken and charred remains of fangs. His skull bones crunched and crackled as he transformed into the misshapen wolf that he had hidden away before. Skin manifested, slithering around his body and encased the gore of his defeat in a fresh naked body. His leg bones pushed outward extending his height by a good two feet. His knees cracked and bent backwards. His feet popped and reformed into massive paws with three-inch claws curling towards the earth. His arms expanded, muscles pulsing and growing beneath the fresh skin and fur.

Juliette's eyes widened as the horror before her took shape. Why couldn't she transform? What power did he hold over her? As he grew, she lost all connection to the ground and continued to fight for every breath, fighting off the invitation of unconsciousness.

The preacher's voice changed from his piercing tenor to a guttural rumble. "You see, you not only come from my brother, but from me. You only transform because I will it, and right now all I will is your feeble death. And here, you thought I was born of you. How pathetic!" His lips restored by the transformation, now stretched wide, exposing the new row of sharp fangs dripping with anticipation of tasting the delicacy hanging from his grip. His thick canine tongue lashed out lapping at the tears streaming down Juliette's cheek. She whimpered. "But before I feast on your friend, I think I'll whet my appetite with you, my little welp."

He squeezed her windpipe, ensuring she couldn't call out as he drew her closer. His jaws opened; the crack of dislocation echoed in Juliette's ears as he maneuvered her entire head in between his teeth. He savored the moment, slowly closing his mouth around her, forcing her to endure each pierce of a fang passing through the skin and into her skull. The taste of blood mingled with her tears, seasoning the kill as her head collapsed under the slow vice-like pressure of his bite. Her blood splashed down his front, spraying her shoes crimson as her body twitched away the last bits of her life.

He crunched on her skull while her body slipped from his grip and crumpled at his feet. He swallowed and lapped at his lips, satisfied but not sated. He picked up Juliette's body and hurled it into the outhouse. He shook off the wave of elation from the fresh infusion of food and transformed back into his human form, Juliette's blood painted down his front.

Showdown

46

Ruby and Ashe put the last of the bottle of whiskey down waiting for Juliette to return with a fresh one. With the hustle and the bustle of the room around them, they had taken little notice of how long she was absent. They had also not detected the tall naked figure drawing so much attention from the rest of the saloon. Ashe saw first. His sudden lack of humor made Ruby stop mid laugh and look up.

"I'm glad you two have found each other. It is so hard to find a soul mate in such a soulless world as ours." Thomas stood tall, not even winded from his feeding on Juliette.

"How the hell are you still alive?" Ashe said, slowly moving his hand to his hip under the table and releasing his gun from its holster.

"Hell is the question, my son." Thomas' hands moved like lightning and with two thick thuds, the gunslinger found himself with a pair of broken bottles protruding from his chest, draining his lungs and his heart of his very life, spilling it out on the full house he had recently played.

"No!" Ruby kicked her chair away and moved to Ashe's side. She placed one hand on his chest and the other caressed his paling cheek.

Ashe struggled to comprehend what was happening. He

figured he would go violently one day, but never had he thought he'd be killed by the preacher from hell while being comforted by his demonic lover.

"I'm fine." Crimson gathered at the corner of his mouth as he worked his tongue to talk. "I just need a second to get my, *cough,* breath." Blood coated the air around the table in a fine mist as he coughed past the gathering blood that filled his lungs, throat and mouth.

"I can't fix this." Ruby said, sincere sympathy in her words.

"Then fuck him up for me, will ya?" Ashe pulled a crooked, pained smile across his lips. Then his head bobbed and sagged down onto his chest, his last breath filled Ruby's nostrils, reminding her of their last night together.

"You know I will, lover." She ran her hand down his cheek, cupped it and filled it with the life leaching out from his body through the bottles. She brought her hands to her mouth and drank, topping her tank with the life blood of her lover. She stood and turned towards Thomas. Her eyes flashed open reflecting the room back at him in their wide onyx glory.

"You have no idea what you've awakened here, do you?" Ruby's voice was cold.

"Oh, I have some idea, my dear. We may be of separate worlds, but we are derived from similar lineages. You from the breast of Lilith and I from the sons of Cain. Our blood runs hot with the death of the world."

"And today mine will run hot with the gush from your dying heart."

"Maybe. But I doubt we'll do much more than raze this backwards town to the ground in our search for revenge. What are you upset about anyway? That I have taken away your cattle? The same creatures you have fed on time and time again. Have you been lulled into thinking you can be accepted by them? That you could even love them?"

"You know nothing of me, old man. Your seed dried up millennia ago and by no fault of mine, I ended up as part of your orbit. A decaying orbit of toxicity and destruction. I may have fed off them, but I never asked for them to worship me. I don't happily take the innocence that they hold dear. It is those things that make me search out the creatures of the night for sustenance. The true evils of this world."

"Spare me. You're no different than I am. Either I kill them, or you do. At the end of the day, they are dust in the ground that you and I tread upon. Why must we continue to waste our energy on a battle that has no end?"

"Oh, it'll have an end today, you son of a bitch."

Ruby burst forward with such speed that even the preacher was taken by surprise. She slammed into his chest, lifting him off his feet and carrying him from the bar, slamming through any obstacle, be it table, supporting beam, or the door frame as she burst from the saloon in a puff of dust and debris. She pushed forward and dug her feet into the ground at the same time, launching Thomas thirty feet into the air. Unholy creature or not, he didn't have the ability to fly. He flailed through the air, his nakedness displayed for the world to see. He arced through the sky and dropped into the livery roof coming to rest in an uncleaned stall. He smashed to the ground atop a pitchfork that lodged itself in his back.

All the way back at the saloon Ruby could hear the angry scream of Thomas as he slid the implement from his back, snapping it over his knee in a petulant fit.

Ruby stood her ground, keeping her eyes open. "What's happening, Ruby?" One of the saloon ladies asked from the Thomas-shaped hole in the front of the building she had just made.

She turned, her true face startling those inside. "Go back

inside!" As she spoke, a blurred red figure sped into her, knocking her back and into the wall of the mercantile across the way. She shook the stars from her gaze and stood, only to be knocked again, the blur flying past in the opposite direction this time. She took flight across the street and into the side of a boarding house. Thomas kept up this barrage for another few passes. Ruby took each hit and gathered her wits. She locked on to him as he gathered momentum for another pass. This time, she acted just in time and braced herself for the impact.

She winced but held her stance as he hit her full force. Her arm connected with his neck, throwing him off balance. He flipped head over heels and skidded to a halt, coming to rest with his head at an odd angle, smashed against the corner of a set of stairs.

Ruby strode to the middle of the street and turned to face him as he shook off the hit. "Enough of the parlor tricks, fucker! Fight me like you think you can win, or are you afraid of a woman's touch?"

Thomas brushed off the dust. He leered at her, his tongue drooped out to the side as he panted and lapped at the small cuts on his face, healing them instantly. "Oh, my child. You have no idea what true suffering is do you? I will enjoy making you beg for me to end it for you. Then I'll make you beg again when I keep you alive for my own fleshly pleasures. Pleasures that you will learn to abhor as I inflict centuries of carnal knowledge onto your supple flesh."

"God, you are full of shit. You think you have anything new to show *me* as far as suffering at the hands of an overconfident and obviously overcompensating," she said, and glanced down at his nakedness with a smirk, "zealot who has no true master other than their own ego? Let's finish this so I can get on with my night, 'cause you're boring me, old man."

"You insolent welp."

"Welp this, motherfucker!"

Ruby dashed towards him, ready to close the gap for a true fight, one she knew she could win if he came close enough. Talons flashed and rang with each connection as each of them parried and lunged and slashed at air that should have been flesh. Their speed was incomprehensible to the onlookers, who saw little more than a moving cloud of dust as the violent ballet proceeded through the street. One would connect, answered by the other slashing at an opening. Their wounds healed almost as fast as they were inflicted. They spun and dodged through building after building, explosions of splinters and dust accentuating every miss and aggravating every hit. If it wasn't for their speed, their epic confrontation would have lasted an hour. Thomas did everything he could to destroy not only Ruby but the town around them, and Ruby worked to contain the conflict to as small an area as possible. He was not going to destroy a town she had learned to be a part of. He was not going to have the satisfaction of standing over her dying body and desecrate it in whatever ways he was inclined. She would keep him moving and wear him down one hit, one slash, one bite at a time.

They burst through the wall of the local newspaper shop, the sound of crunching metal following them out as the printing press collapsed on itself after being the backdrop for their violent exchange.

Ruby kicked forward and sent Thomas reeling into the middle of the street. She was winded but still standing. He, on the other hand, was showing some fatigue, taking longer to recover from blows and wounds. He was on all fours panting, blood dripping from his sagging body. Ruby stood just ten feet from him, with mussed hair and tatter clothes but focused on victory.

"Come on, old man. I thought you had something to teach me. Where's your bravado now?"

"Bitch!" He spat a stream of blood and glared up at her as he raised himself, still panting but readying himself for another assault.

"That's not the safe word, honey." Ruby grinned a wicked smile and took a stride towards him.

He stood, fists at his side and glaring as Ruby neared. He flung one fist forward and a cloud of dust smacked her in the face, filling her eyes with dirt. Taken off guard, she instinctively put her hands to her eyes, rubbing at the irritating grit that assaulted her eyeballs. As she struggled, Thomas went for broke. He slashed and punched and kicked and landed as many blows to Ruby as he could while she struggled to recover from his cheap shot. Ruby squinted past the pain and saw the combination of moves he was enlisting. She gritted her teeth, kept her eyes as open as she could and intercepted his next blow.

His arm landed on her side, and she locked it in place by bringing her arm down and lifting up. Thomas yelped as his elbow inverted with a snap. He swung his other arm, and she captured that as well and dislocated it with a quick upward motion. Ruby flung her head forward, smashing her forehead into his nose. A stream of blood painted the dirt street between them. Ruby let loose his limply swinging arms and kicked out, landing her hit just under his sternum. Thomas flew backwards ten feet and smacked face first into the ground. He grumbled on the ground searching for the strength to continue.

Ruby strode forward, plumes of dust rising with every deliberate step. She was tired of the games and the arrogance of this lesser creature. He was a true believer in the fact that this world was his to play in. The trouble was that this world was filled with many creatures. Some strong, some weak. But without an acceptance of your place in the world and an appreciation for the creativity and autonomy of others, you were nothing more than a bully and a false idol.

Ruby grabbed hold of the groaning man's wispy gray tuft of hair and lifted him. He was still healing slowly. She held him up. "This is for Juliette." She kicked down and obliterated his right knee. The crack was heard in the saloon where the onlookers winced at the thunderclap that Ruby had elicited from such a small joint. "And this… is for Ashe." She kicked out his other knee, sending him to rest painfully on the useless joints.

He panted and yelled in pain as he gathered his words. "You think you have beat me, Jezebel? You think they will accept you after this? You have lost everything and even if you kill me, I will go…"

Ruby plunged her fist into his mouth, grasping his writhing, wriggling tongue from its perch and with a yank, plucked it from his head. She held it in front of his wide eyes;

"I'm sorry, you were saying?"

She was answered with a gurgled spurt of astonishment from Thomas.

Ruby dropped the tongue in the dirt and stomped it flat. She grabbed his bottom teeth with one hand and his top with the other and in one violent motion the top of his head was flung backwards, hanging loose at the base of his skull. She reached down into his neck, the rest of his useless body struggling to fight off the inevitable. She snaked her hand deep into his abyss, latched onto his beating heart and closed her fist around it. She leaned down to look into his upside-down eyes. "Now I lay YOU down to sleep, preacher." She pulled his misshapen heart loose from its connections to the rest of his body. His desperate eyes searched for a solution to his problem, until she presented it with his own heart, giving it a playful lick, before her monstrous maw expanded and she placed the dying heart onto the bottom row of her teeth and with a slow motion, made him watch as she clamped down, squishing the final beats out and swallowing the decrepit, deceitful, aged soul. His eyes flickered with the final twitches of life and his whole body went limp. For good measure, she slashed his throat and alleviated his body of its head. She picked up the head and took a slow walk to the burn pile to ensure that, this time, he wasn't coming back.

47

Ruby stood over the cold bodies of her dead friends laid out in the street. Juliette's petite figure, hands clasped demurely at her belly. Her shoulders were absent their centerpiece. Ashe's crisp white shirt, now decorated with the two drooping roses of red that stained his chest. Both had been carried out to the street and laid to rest in wait of the coffin maker to accommodate their next stage of the journey to the grave.

"Do they need headstones, ma'am?" The town doctor had prepped the bodies for the grave. He stood next to Ruby, a dark suit with a gently wrinkled jacket draped over his hunched shoulders.

"I don't think that's necessary. Neither of them is from around here, and I don't believe anyone will come looking for them." She pulled her sadness back into the recess of her heart, stood tall and turned to walk away. "Just make sure they have a nice view, will ya?"

The somber man nodded, his stovepipe hat accenting his response as Ruby walked away.

* * *

* * *

Ruby took her time getting packed. She was disappointed that she would not be staying here, but the town had changed too much in such a short time after the death of Brother Thomas.

The townsfolk banded together to consecrate the ruins of the church by burning its remains to the ground. In its place, a tree was planted as a symbol of growth for the rapidly changing township.

The railroad workers filed in and filled any empty space, erecting tents and temporary businesses on the outskirts of the town. The influx of people and money meant a bustle of fresh construction, new faces, and new opportunities for the townsfolk to take advantage of and to be corrupted by. Work had already begun to repair the damage to the saloon inflicted by Ruby and Thomas' melee. Few words were spoken about those last few days of violence and cleansing. Instead, the folks of the small town did what they do best, buried the past, covered up the bruises and the scars and moved on from the unpleasant memories.

Ruby could be welcomed into the new façade, but she would never feel at home without Hank, Ashe, or Juliette. It was better for her to find another perch to call home and let the morbid memories that accompanied her to be buried with her friends on the hill outside town.

Ruby booked a ticket west on the next stagecoach and prepared herself to travel. One difference she had noticed since dispatching the preacher was that her hunger had waned, much as it did when she found herself in the possession of her prized vampire's teeth. Since devouring the preacher's heart, she had felt anew. Her hair had its young luster again, her skin was taught, and she felt her full power surge. She was unsure how long this would last, but she had a feeling it would be with her for some time, allowing her to travel and find a new home without the anticipation of regressing again. Her days of feeding on vampires was not over, however. They still held a place in her gullet for the hunt and power they provided, but she felt no urgency to sate those urges.

Her clothes packed away, Ruby stood at the foot of her bed staring at her procured mementos from Ashe and Juliette. A silver mirror and a pocket watch stared up at her, awaiting their turn to be packed away for the trip ahead. She ran a finger around the face of the mirror, its contours gripping at her fingertip as she pulled it down the intricate design work. She smiled gently, and lifted it into her bag, placed neatly amongst her clothes to pad its journey. The watch, she lifted by its chain and slid the bulbous body into a slim pocket on the front of her dress, securing the end of the chain to her bodice with a pin. She would leave the chest and her bag for the boy downstairs to cart down to the coach while she made her goodbyes with the remaining ladies that were left in charge of the saloon.

She glided down the curved staircase, exchanged bawdy repartee with the ladies, snatched a bottle of Hank's finest for the travel and was off.

* * *

The coach clattered to a halt, its energetic steeds whinnying with appreciation for the short respite. Ruby directed the driver's young assistant to her luggage and made her way to the open door to claim her seat for the long ride.

She settled into the seat opposite a single other rider. She smoothed out the pleats in her dress and brushed a fine layer of dust from the hem. Her eyes took in the view of the other passenger and followed his line up from the tip of his well-worn black boots, crisp black pants, a black duster lain across his lap hiding away his gun belt and the knife sheath strapped to his thigh. He wore a crisp, laundered black shirt and his head was tilted down as he seemed to be napping.

Something was familiar about this man. His smell, his build, and even his clothes reminded her of someone from not too long ago.

"Hello Ruby. It's been a while." The man gently lifted his head; long dark locks draped over his shoulders. His chin appeared with a couple days' worth of stubble. A gentle smile was draped across his lips. Ruby met his dark eyes with a mischievous glint.

"I knew I had picked the right carriage. Mind a bit of company, Finn?"

The door closed and the coachman berated his young helper as he climbed up into the shotgun seat. With a quick snap of the reins, they were off, a cloud of soft earth pluming up from the steel and wood wheels as they chased the setting sun out of town.

The End

About the Author

Author and musician, John Dover, Lives in Portland Oregon with his wife Jessica and their dog, Lulu. John began his writing career around 2012 with his Johnny Scotch series of books and comic book. Soon John was published in multiple horror anthologies and continued his work on creating longer works. In 2021, he wrote, *Once Upon a Fang in the West,* his introduction into the Wild West world blending horror with his appreciation for the Spaghetti Western genre of movies.

As a musician, John maintains a studio of private students, performs with Ben Rice and the PDX Hustle, Bridge City Brass, and others, along with his freelance work in and around Portland and the Pacific Northwest. He has also blended his writing and music by producing a trumpet method book and a series of collaborative songs and accompanied spoken word pieces that he uses to reach wider audiences and to bring people into his creative worlds.

Special Thanks

Special thanks go out to my wife Jessica. Though I mention it in my dedication, the support that I see on a daily basis is overwhelming. Your hard work and dedication to your own craft and interests gives me strength and drive when the tank feels near empty.

Thanks to Charles Austin Muir. You have stuck with me through two books in this wild world. Your attention to detail and willingness to see my work for more than it may appear at times truly helps to bring the best out in my words.

Thanks also to Gary Brown for helping to usher the final edits across the finish line.

Thank you to Don Aguillo. Your vision to bring my words into the visual medium is astounding. I am honored that your art greets readers as they venture into my writing.

Finally, thanks to all the readers that take the time to visit my world and let me take them on adventures time and time again. An author is nothing without the ones that crack the spine and delve into the twisted worlds that we craft.

www.ingramcontent.com/pod-product-compliance
Lightning Source LLC
LaVergne TN
LVHW090514110826
845146LV00003B/849